Plaza Suite

A COMEDY IN THREE ACTS

By Neil Simon

SAMUEL FRENCH, INC.

45 WEST 25TH STREET   NEW YORK 10010

7623 SUNSET BOULEVARD   HOLLYWOOD 90046

LONDON   TORONTO

PLAZA SUITE, by Neil Simon, was first presented by Saint-Subber at the Plymouth Theater, New York City, on February 14, 1968 with the following cast:

VISITOR FROM MAMARONECK

Bellhop.....................................Bob Balaban
Karen Nash....................Maureen Stapleton
Sam Nash...........................George C. Scott
Waiter...Jose Ocasio
Jean McCormack..............Claudette Nevins

VISITOR FROM HOLLYWOOD

Waiter...Jose Ocasio
Jesse Kiplinger....................George C. Scott
Muriel Tate.....................Maureen Stapleton

VISITOR FROM FOREST HILLS

Norma Hubley................Maureen Stapleton
Roy Hubley..........................George C. Scott
Bordon Eisler............................Bob Balaban
Mimsey Hubley................Claudette Nevins

Directed by Mike Nichols

These are three plays all taking place in the same suite at the Plaza hotel.

VISITOR FROM MAMARONECK

CAST

KAREN NASH

SAM NASH

BELLHOP

WAITER

JEAN MCCORMACK

ACT ONE

SCENE: *A suite at the Plaza Hotel. The seventh floor over-looking the park. The set is divided into two rooms. The room at Stage Right is the living room. It is a well-appointed room, tastefully furnished with an entrance door at extreme Right and windows that look out over the park. A door leads into the bed-room, which has a large double bed, etc., and a door that leads to the bathroom. The room also contains a large closet.*

TIME: *About four in the afternoon, mid-December.*

AT RISE: *The door of the suite opens and a BELLHOP enters and switches on the LIGHTS in the living room. He carries one small overnight bag. KAREN NASH enters behind him. She wears a six-year-old mink coat which could use a bit of restyling, and a pair of galoshes. Underneath she wears an expensive suit which unfortunately looked better on the model in Bendel's than it does on KAREN. KAREN is forty-eight years old, and she makes no bones about it. C'est la vie. She is a pleasant affable woman who has let weight and age take their natural course. A mink hat is plopped down on her head. She carries a box from Bendel's with her afternoon's purchases, and a small bouquet of flowers. The BOY closes a half-open window in the living room, and puts the bag on the luggage tray. KAREN looks around the living room, crosses to bedroom and puts her packages down on a chair. The BOY goes to bathroom and turns LIGHT on in there. KAREN follows the BOY to the bathroom. The BOY comes out of the bathroom, crosses living room, opens door to leave, and hesitates in the door-way.*

BELLHOP. Everything all right, m'am?

KAREN. Wait a minute, I want to make sure this is the right room. (*She crosses back into the living room.*) I know this is Suite 719, but was it always 719?

BELLHOP. Yes, m'am. 719.

KAREN. No, you don't understand. I know sometimes hotels change the numbers around and this could have been 723 or 715. And it's very important I get 719. (*She returns to bedroom for flowers.*)

BELLHOP. I'm here two years, it's always been 719.

KAREN. Because you know about 826 at the Savoy-Plaza?

BELLHOP. No, m'am.

KAREN. (*Unwrapping flowers at table behind the sofa in living room.*) Oh, well, they had a famous murder in 826. Then the next year there was a fire and the year after that a husband and a wife committed suicide. Then no one wanted 826. So they turned it into a linen closet. It's a fact, there is no more 826 at the Savoy-Plaza.

BELLHOP. There's no more Savoy-Plaza either. They tore it down two years ago.

KAREN. (*Looks at him incredulously, then goes to look out window.*) Oh, my God, look at that. There's no Savoy-Plaza . . . What's that monstrosity?

BELLHOP. It's the new General Motors building.

KAREN. (*Still looking out window.*) Shows you how often I get into the city. Well, listen, that's what they're doing today. If it's old and it's beautiful, it's not there in the morning . . .

BELLHOP. (*Indicating other windows.*) Well, you still have a nice view from here.

KAREN. (*Crosses to other windows and looks out.*) Mmm, for how long? I guarantee you Central Park comes down in five years.

BELLHOP. You think so?

KAREN. (*Starts to put flowers in vase on sofa table.*) I *know* so. Five years from now you'll look out this window and you'll see one little tree and the world's largest A & P.

BELLHOP. I don't think I'll be working here five years from now.

KAREN. You mean the rumor is true?

BELLHOP. What rumor?

KAREN. That the Plaza is coming down too!

BELLHOP. *This* Plaza?

KAREN. (*Puts vase on chest between the windows.*) I don't want to worry you or anything. It's just a rumor. No one knows for sure . . . But it's definitely coming down.

BELLHOP. I didn't hear that.

KAREN. (*Crossing to bedroom, takes bag from luggage rack and puts it on dresser in front of bedroom window.*) Well, I'm sure they want to keep it quiet from the staff. The story is that they're going to tear down the Plaza and put up a fifty-two-story luxury hotel.

BELLHOP. Why? *This* is a luxury hotel.

KAREN. Yeah, but it's an *old* luxury hotel. Today it has to be new. Old is no good any more. (*Picks up phone on chest in living room.*) Well, all I really care about is tonight.

BELLHOP. Yes, m'am. Is there anything else?

KAREN. Oh, wait a minute. (*She puts down phone, runs to bedroom for her purse, and looks for change.*) Don't tell me I don't have any change.

BELLHOP. That's all right, m'am.

KAREN. (*Crossing back into living room.*) It's not all right. This is your living. (*Takes out a dollar bill.*) Here you are.

BELLHOP. (*Taking it.*) Thank you very much.

KAREN. I'll be very honest with you. I don't usually give dollar tips. But it's my anniversary. So I can be a sport.

BELLHOP. (*Hand on door. He'd really like to go.*) Oh, well, congratulations.

KAREN. Thank you, dear. Twenty-four years ago tonight I spent my honeymoon in this room. This *is* 719, isn't it?

BELLHOP. Yes, m'am. 719.

KAREN. I bet you weren't even born twenty-four years ago, right?

BELLHOP. No, I was born . . .

KAREN. You know what I was? I was twenty-five. You know what that makes me today? . . . Some old lady.

BELLHOP. Well, you certainly don't look like an old lady. (*Smiles.*) Well . . . have a pleasant stay, m'am . . . and happy anniversary. (*He starts out door.*)

KAREN. Thank you, dear . . . and take my advice. Don't rush . . . but look around for another job. (*The* BOY *nods and exits.* KAREN *crosses to the bedroom, and looks at herself in the full length mirror on the closet door. Takes off hat and puts it on the dresser.*) You are definitely some old lady. (*She crosses to phone on night table next to bed, takes it and sits on bed, still wearing her mink coat.*) Room service, please. (*She groans as she bends over to take off galoshes.*) Ohhhhh . . . (*Into phone.*) No, operator. I was groaning to myself . . . (*Taking off her coat.*) Hello, room service? . . . Listen, room service, this is Mrs. Sam Nash in Suite 719 . . . I would like a nice, cold bottle of champagne . . . That sounds good, is it French? . . . Fine . . . with two glasses and a tray of assorted hors d'oeuvres . . . but listen, room service, I don't want any anchovies . . . They always give you anchovy patties with the hors d'oeuvres and my husband doesn't eat anchovies and I hate them so don't give me any anchovies . . . Instead of the anchovies, give me some extra smoked salmon or you can split them up . . . half smoked salmon and half caviars . . . That's right. Mrs. Nash. 719 . . . No anchovies . . . (*She hangs up.*) They'll give me anchovies. (*She puts phone back on night table.*) Look at that. No more Savoy-Plaza. (*Starts to take off galoshes again. The TELEPHONE rings. There is one in each room. She gets up and picks up the one next to bed.*) Hello . . . (*The PHONE in the living room*

*rings again. Hastily she hangs up the bedroom phone and
rushes to answer it.*) Hello? . . . Oh, Sam. Where are
you? . . . Good. Come up. I'm here . . . What room do
you think? . . . 719 . . . Remember? 719? Suite 719?
. . . That's right! (*She hangs up.*) He doesn't remember . . . (*She rushes to Bendel box and takes out a sheer
negligee. She crosses to mirror on closet door, and looks
at herself with negligee in front of her. She is not completely enchanted. The TELEPHONE rings. She puts
down negligee and rushes to living room to answer it.*)
Hello . . . (*The PHONE in the bedroom rings again.
She hastily hangs up the living room phone and rushes to
answer it.*) Hello? . . . Oh, hello, Miss McCormack. . . .
No, he's not, dear. He's on his way up. Yes, I will . . .
It's not important, is it? . . . Well, he seemed so tired
lately, I was hoping he wouldn't have to think about work
tonight. (*Glancing down at her feet.*) Oh, my God, I still
have my galoshes on . . . All right, I'll tell him to call.
Yes, when he comes in. Goodbye. (*She hangs up and
quickly bends over in an effort to remove her galoshes.
She is having difficulty. The DOORBELL rings.*) Oh,
dammit. (*Calls out.*) Just a minute! (*The DOORBELL
rings again. She is having much trouble with the right
galosh.*) You had to wear galoshes today, right? (*She
pulls her right galosh off but her shoe remains in it. The
DOORBELL rings impatiently.*) Oh, for God's sakes . . .
(*She tries to pull her shoe out of the galosh but it is im-
bedded in there.*) All right, all right, I'm coming. (*She
throws down galosh with shoe still in it and "limps" across
the room in one galosh and her stockinged foot. She
crosses into living room.*) Look at this, my twenty-fourth
anniversary. (*She "limps" to the door and opens it.* SAM
NASH *stands there.* SAM *has just turned fifty but has made
every effort to conceal it. He is trim, impeccably neat. His
clothes are well-tailored, although a bit on the junior executive side. He carries an attaché case, a fine leather
Gucci product. Everything about* SAM *is measured, efficient, economic. Smiles warmly.*) Hello, Sam.

(SAM *walks brusquely past her, surveying room.*)

SAM. An hour and fifteen minutes I was in the God-damned dentist's chair . . . (*He puts down attaché case on chair Downstage of door to bedroom, and takes off coat.*)

KAREN. (*Closes door, still warmly.*) How do you feel, Sam?

SAM. Between his lousy dirty jokes and WQXR-FM, I got some headache. (*He crosses to mirror over chest in living room and looks at his teeth.*) Did anyone call?

KAREN. Sam, do you remember this room? (*Moving to him.*)

SAM. (*Still examining teeth.*) Well, two more caps and I'm through. (*He turns, baring his teeth at her.*) What do you think?

KAREN. (*Puts her hands in front of her eyes to shield the glare.*) Ooh, dazzling!

SAM. You don't think they're too white, do you? (*Turns and looks in mirror again.*) Do they look too white to you?

KAREN. No, no. Perfect. Very nice with the blue shirt.

SAM. (*Still looking.*) These don't stain, you know. A hundred years from now when I'm dead and buried, they'll be the same color.

KAREN. Oh, good. You'll look wonderful. You don't remember this room, do you?

SAM. (*Looks at watch.*) Four-thirty already? The meeting must be over . . . Didn't anyone call? (*Takes coat and attaché case into bedroom, putting the coat on the chest and the case on the bed.*)

KAREN. Miss McCormack, from the office . . . She wants you to call back.

SAM. (*Looks at her annoyed.*) Why didn't you tell me?

KAREN. We were busy talking about your white teeth. Happy anniversary, Sam. (*Picks up vase and crosses to bedroom.*)

SAM. (*Not hearing her, into phone.*) Judson 6-5900

. . . What did you say? (*Sees her limp into bedroom.*) What's the matter with your leg?

KAREN. (*Limps into bathroom.*) One is shorter than the other. Didn't you ever notice that? I've had it for years.

SAM. (*Into phone.*) Lorainne? Mr. Nash. Let me have Miss McCormack, please. (SAM *looks at himself in closet mirror.*) Well, that kills my barber's appointment today. Oh, could I use five minutes under the sun lamp. (*Into phone.* KAREN *begins to sing in bathroom.*) Miss Mc-Cormack? . . . Did Henderson call? . . . Did he send the contracts? (*Places hand over ear to shut out singing.*) What about Nizer? . . . I see . . . (*He quickly takes a note pad from night table and places it on the attaché case on the bed in front of him. He can't find a pencil. He snaps fingers at* KAREN. *Still into phone.*) What does it look like? . . . Ah huh . . . ah huh . . . (*He snaps fingers at* KAREN *again.*) A pencil . . . pencil . . . (KAREN, *rushing in from bathroom, searches through the night tables on both sides of the bed and dresser.* SAM *still on phone.*) Very good. All right, give me the figures. (*He nods into phone.* KAREN *still can't find a pencil. She limps hurriedly over to her purse on the sofa table in the living room. Into phone.*) It sounds right but I've got to go over the estimates . . . Tomorrow morning? That doesn't give us much time . . . Wait a minute, give me those figures again . . . (*Hand over phone, he whispers angrily.*) Karen, for God's sakes, a pencil! (KAREN *is frantically looking through her purse. Into phone.*) One seventy-five escalating up to three and a quarter . . . (KAREN *takes a lipstick out of her purse and hobbles quickly to* SAM. *She hands it to him.*) Hold it. (*He writes on pad.*) One seventy-five up to three and a quarter . . . (*He stops writing and looks at* KAREN.) That's a lipstick.

KAREN. (*Taking empty Bendel box from chair.*) I don't have a pencil.

SAM. Then why do you give me a lipstick?

KAREN. Because I don't have a pencil. It's Shocking

Pink but it writes. (*Puts box into wastebasket next to dresser.*)

SAM. (*He glares at her. Into phone.*) All right, I'm going to go over my figures here. If Henderson calls or the contracts come in, bring them right over. What's that? (*He laughs.*) Yes! Well, it's like we were saying the other night, it's the old badger game. (*He laughs again.* KAREN *mocks his private joke with* MISS MCCORMACK *as she hobbles back into bedroom.*) All right, I'll speak to you later. And thank you, Miss McCormack. (*He hangs up.*) A hundred and seventy-five thousand dollar contract, you give me a lipstick. (*Puts lipstick down on table next to chair.*)

KAREN. (*Hobbles out of bathroom with vase.*) I'd have given you blood but it isn't blue.

SAM. All right, don't test me because I've got enough of a headache. (*He rubs eyes with thumb and index finger, opens case and takes out bottle of aspirin. She limps into living room and places vase on desk. He looks at her.*) And for God's sakes, Karen, stop hobbling around. I don't feel like listening to thump thump thump!

KAREN. (*She sighs.*) And happy anniversary to you.

SAM. What?

KAREN. Forget it. (*Sits at desk and takes off other galosh and shoe.*)

SAM. (*Moving to bathroom with aspirin.*) What are you talking about? . . . It's not our anniversary.

KAREN. Today is December 14th, isn't it?

SAM. Yes.

KAREN. So. We're married twenty-four years today.

SAM. (*Looks at her incredulously.*) Are you serious?

KAREN. We're not married twenty-four years today?

SAM. No. (*Comes out of bathroom with glass of water and takes aspirin.*)

KAREN. We're not married twenty-four years?

SAM. No.

KAREN. We're not married?

SAM. Tomorrow is our anniversary and we're married

twenty-three years. (*Puts glass down on dresser and moves into the living room.*)

KAREN. (*Looks at him.*) Are you sure?

SAM. What do you mean, am I sure? I know when our anniversary is. December 15th, we're married twenty-three years. How can you make a mistake like that?

KAREN. All right, don't get so excited and it's not such a big mistake because I didn't get you a present . . . You're sure it's not the 14th?

SAM. I go through this with you every year. When it comes to money or dates or ages, you are absolutely unbelievable. (*Turns, exasperated, and goes to bedroom.*) We were married December 15th, 1945—

KAREN. Then I'm right. Twenty-*four* years.

SAM. 45 from 68 is *23!*

KAREN. Then I'm wrong. (*Shrugs.*) Math isn't one of my best subjects.

SAM. (*Hanging jacket over dresser chair.*) This isn't math, this is people's *lives!* (*Moves back to* KAREN.) How old are you?

KAREN. What?

SAM. It's a simple question. How old are you?

KAREN. (*She's reluctant to answer, moves to window.*) I don't want to play.

SAM. I can't believe it. You really don't know how old you are.

KAREN. I know how old I am. But you get me nervous. Promise you won't leave me if I'm wrong . . . I'll be 49 in April. (SAM *stares at her in disbelief, crosses back into bedroom and wearily leans against closet door.* KAREN *follows him.*) Isn't that right?

SAM. No, but you're close.

KAREN. I'm not going to be 49?

SAM. Not *this* April. *This* April you're going to be 48. How the hell can you make a mistake like that? Can't you add? (*Taking several contracts out of attaché case.*)

KAREN. All right, don't talk to me like I'm a child. I'm a 48-year-old woman.

SAM. But the thing that infuriates me is that you make the mistake the wrong way. Why don't you make yourself younger instead of older, the way other women do?

KAREN. Okay, I'm 47. (*Throws herself on bed and poses sexily.*) So how do I look to you now?

SAM. I've got work to do. I've got a very important meeting at eight o'clock in the morning. (*Crosses to desk and sits.*)

KAREN. (*Sitting up in bed.*) Oh, come on, Sam, where's your sense of humor? I think it's cute as hell that I don't know how old I am.

SAM. (*Starts to look over papers.*) I can't even think straight. I've had five meetings this morning, four teeth capped and I haven't even had my metracal. (*He crosses to phone in living room.*) I'd better eat something. (*Picks up phone.*)

KAREN. I just ordered hors d'oeuvres.

SAM. Not for me. You know I'm on nine hundred calories a day. (*Into phone.*) Room service, please. (*He turns and looks in mirror.*) My God, who the hell is that? Will you look at my eyes? I have no pupils left. (*He turns to* KAREN.) Come here. Look at this. Do you see any pupils?

KAREN. (*Crosses and looks into mirror.*) Yes, Sam. I see two gorgeous pupils . . .

SAM. (*Still in mirror.*) Where? Where? I don't have a pupil in my head. Would you get my eye drops out of the case?

KAREN. (*Crossing to case on bed.*) I think you've been overworking, Sam. I haven't seen you two nights this month.

SAM. (*Stretches arms.*) I really could use some sun. And about a month of sleep.

KAREN. (*Searching through case.*) Hey, why don't we go down to Jamaica for a couple weeks? Just the two of us. We haven't done that in years.

SAM. (*Into phone, pacing.*) Oh, hello, room service, where were you? . . . Listen, I'd like a plate of cold roast beef, medium rare, very lean. You know what very lean is? . . . No, it doesn't mean no fat . . . It means *absolutely* no fat . . . and I want a salad, *no dressing,* a half grapefruit and a pot of black coffee . . . And I'd appreciate it as soon as possible . . . Wait a second. (*To* KAREN, *who has entered living room with eye drops.*) Where are we again?

KAREN. 719, Plaza Hotel, New York 23, New York.

SAM. (*Into phone.*) 719 . . . As soon as you can. (*He hangs up, moves down to* KAREN *at couch.*) What's wrong with you today?

KAREN. You wouldn't believe it, but fifteen minutes ago I was the happiest woman on earth . . . Sit down, I'll put your pupils back in.

SAM. (*Hand extended.*) I can do it myself.

KAREN. I know you can, Sam, but I *like* to put your eye drops in. (*He lies down on sofa with head on arm and she moves to look down at him from side of sofa.*) It's the only time lately you look at me. (*She poises eye dropper.*)

SAM. (*Looks up at her.*) I'm sorry.

KAREN. You are?

SAM. I haven't been nice to *anyone* the past couple of weeks.

KAREN. You sounded swell to Miss McCormack.

SAM. Put the eye drops in.

KAREN. (*Bending down over arm of sofa.*) First give an old lady a kiss.

(*He gives her a soft, gentle kiss.*)

SAM. I give you my permission to hate me.

KAREN. (*Straightens up.*) I'll save it for later. Open your gorgeous pupils. (KAREN *fills dropper with fluid.*)

SAM. Eight months I've been working on this deal and suddenly today my two top men in the office come down with the flu and I've got to do everything myself. (*She puts drops in eye. He jumps up.*) AAGHH! (*He grabs eye in pain.*)

KAREN. What's the matter?

SAM. (*Sitting up.*) You *drop* them in, you don't *push* them in.

KAREN. I'm sorry, you moved your head.

SAM. I moved my head because you were stabbing my eyeball. (*Gets up and peers in mirror over fireplace.*) Oh, dammit!

KAREN. All right, don't panic, Sam, I'm sorry.

SAM. Why do you think they call it a dropper? If they wanted you to stab people they would call it a stabber. (*Grabs it from her.*) Give it to me, I'll do it myself. (*Lies back down on sofa and begins to put drops in both eyes.*)

KAREN. You mean that's the end of being nice to each other?

SAM. I don't know what we're doing in a hotel anyway.

KAREN. What's the Plaza got to do with my stabbing your eyeball?

SAM. Because it's insane being here, that's why. I've got work to do tonight, I don't know how I'm going to concentrate.

KAREN. You've got to sleep *some* place tonight. The painter says it's going to take two days for the house to dry.

SAM. Yes, but why *now?* Do it in the spring. This is my busy time of the year. (SAM *puts eye drops on the coffee table and crosses to bedroom.*)

KAREN. I know, but it's not the painter's busy time of the year. In the spring he doesn't want to know you.

SAM. Why didn't you ask me first?

KAREN. (*She follows him into bedroom.*) I never see you . . . I saw the painter.

SAM. You could have checked with my secretary. (*He goes into bathroom.*)

KAREN. I did. She said go ahead and paint the house. (*She takes coat from bed and hangs it in closet.*)

SAM'S VOICE. Of all times of the year. Did you bring my things? Toothbrush? Pajamas?

KAREN. I brought your toothbrush.

SAM's VOICE. You forgot my pajamas?

KAREN. (*Plops down on bed.*) I didn't forget them, I just didn't bring them.

SAM. (*He comes out of bathroom wiping eyes on towel.*) Why not?

KAREN. Because this is Suite 719 at the Plaza and I just didn't think you'd want your pajamas tonight.

SAM. You know I can't sleep without pajamas (*He returns to bathroom.*)

KAREN. (*Yelling after him.*) I took that into consideration . . .

SAM's VOICE. What?

KAREN. Never mind. They've got shops in the lobby. (*Gets up and picks up phone next to bed.*) Should I send for their catalogue or will you take pot luck?

SAM's VOICE. Heh. You know what a pair of pajamas would cost at the Plaza? Forty, fifty dollars.

KAREN. You want me to send a bellhop to Bloomingdale's? (*Hangs up phone.*)

SAM. (*Comes out of bathroom.*) I don't understand you. One lousy little bag is all you had to pack.

KAREN. Forgive me. It's my busy time of the year.

SAM. Karen, do me a favor. Don't get brittle. (SAM *crosses to desk in living room.*) I'm very shaky right now and one good crack and I go right to the dry cleaners . . . Boy, could I use a nice, big, cold double martini. (*He sits and begins to examine contracts.*)

KAREN. (*Follows him into living room and leans on the chest of drawers.*) Don't get angry but can I make a suggestion? Why don't you have a nice, big, cold double martini?

SAM. Are you serious? You know how many calories are in a double martini?

KAREN. (*Shrugs.*) Four or five million?

SAM. You know my metabolism. One double martini and right in front of your eyes I get flabby.

KAREN. You used to get sexy. (*She takes a sheet from pile of stationery in the chest.*)

SAM. (*Gets up with papers to sit in more comfort on sofa.*) Well, now I get flabby. Unless I watch myself like a hawk . . . (*As he passes fireplace mirror, he pauses, admiring waistline.*) which I think I manage to do. (*Sits on sofa.*)

KAREN. (*She starts to fold the piece of stationery.*) I like you flabby.

SAM. What does that mean?

KAREN. (*Still folding paper.*) It means I like you flabby. I admit you look like one of the Pepsi generation but it seems a little unnatural to me. A man of your age ought to have a couple of pounds of skin hanging over his belt.

SAM. Well, I'm sorry to disappoint you.

KAREN. I'm not disappointed, I'm uncomfortable. I watch you when you get undressed at night. Nothing moves. You're vacuum packed. When you open your belt I expect it to go like a can of coffee— Pzzzzzz! (*She continues folding.*)

SAM. Do you think it's easy with my metabolism to keep my weight down? Do you know what it's like to have a business luncheon at the Villa Capri and watch someone slop down a bowl of spaghetti and I'm munching on a hearts of lettuce salad?

KAREN. My compliments to your restraint.

SAM. I go through torture to maintain my weight.

KAREN. I have nothing but admiration for your waistline. (*She is through folding.*)

SAM. But you like me flabby.

KAREN. We all have our little perversions.

SAM. Can we drop the subject?

KAREN. Like a baked potato.

SAM. Thank you.

KAREN. You're welcome. (*She aims her finished paper airplane across the room and lets it fly.*)

SAM. (*Gets up and paces angrily.*) Why do you like me flabby?

KAREN. Is the floor open again?

SAM. No. Forget it.

KAREN. It's forgotten.

SAM. What was I just doing?

KAREN. Watching yourself like a hawk. (*She crosses to bedroom and begins to fold negligee at dresser.*)

SAM. (*He returns to the sofa. There is a silence. Finally.*) Look, I just want to say one more thing and then the discussion is closed. (KAREN *puts down negligee and crosses back to sofa in living room.*) I'm at the athletic club three, four times a week watching men at least ten years younger than me huffing and puffing trying to sweat off a couple of ounces that goes right back on after the cocktail hour. Now maybe you don't consider it a monumental achievement, but my weight hasn't changed in six years. I'm still one seventy-seven on the scale.

KAREN. So am I. (*Crosses to bedroom, and puts negligee away in chest.*) Now you know why I like you flabby . . . The subject is closed. (*She crosses to chair and sits.*)

SAM. (*Upset, he remains in living room. They contemplate the floor a few seconds.*) Hey, Karen.

KAREN. Yah, Sam . . .

SAM. Let's not fight.

KAREN. It's all right with me, Sam.

SAM. Let's be nice to each other.

KAREN. Okay . . . Who goes first?

SAM. (*He gets up and starts for bedroom. He stops at the door, trying to find words.*) Karen . . .

KAREN. (*Looks up.*) Yes, Sam?

SAM. (*This doesn't seem to be the time to bring up whatever is on his mind.*) Nothing . . . I'm going to do a little work, okay? (*He goes back into living room and sits on sofa.*)

KAREN. (*Still sitting. Without malice.*) You don't even remember this room, you louse.

SAM. What's that?

KAREN. (*Gets up and crosses into living room.*) I may not know how old I am but I sure as hell remember we spent our honeymoon night in Suite 719 at the Plaza Hotel and this is definitely 719 because I just tipped the bellhop an entire dollar.

SAM. (*Looks at room for the first time.*) Was this the room?

KAREN. Oh, Christ. (*She sits on the arm of the sofa.*)

SAM. (*Gets up and looks about.*) Wait a minute, I think you're right. (*He looks into bedroom.*) Sure, this looks like the suite. Only it was decorated differently. This room was blue.

KAREN. (*Going into bedroom.*) That was you. You were in the Navy. The bedroom was green.

SAM. I think you're mistaken. The bedroom was blue.

KAREN. You're probably confusing it with some other honeymoon . . . (*Sitting on bed.*) Hey, Sam, remember we had dinner here in the bedroom?

SAM. No.

KAREN. Yes. We had dinner here in the bedroom. Do you remember what we had?

SAM. For dinner? Twenty-three years ago?

KAREN *I* remember. You remember too. Take a guess.

SAM. Karen, I don't remember.

KAREN. Yes, you do. Think about it a second.

SAM. I thought about it. I don't remember.

KAREN. We had a bottle of champagne and a tray full of hors d'oeuvres. And we left all the anchovies in the drawer. (*Indicates night table.*)

SAM. Oh. (*Crosses and looks out living room window.*)

KAREN. See. It's coming back to you. (*Notices him looking out window.*) If you're looking for the Savoy-Plaza, it's not there. (*She goes to bedroom window and follows his gaze.*)

SAM. (*Looking out window.*) I'm looking at the Pierre.

KAREN. There it is.

SAM. . . . Karen.

KAREN. What?

SAM. (*Still looking out window.*) It was 819. (KAREN *steps back from window and looks at* SAM. SAM *turns and looks at her.*) We were in 819, not 719.

KAREN. (*She glares at him and grits her teeth with hostility.*) You're wrong!

SAM. I'm not wrong, I'm right. We were in 819. I'm right.

KAREN. (*Angry.*) Don't keep saying you're right like you're right. You're wrong. We were in 719.

SAM. I'll prove it to you. Come here. (KAREN *joins him at living room window.*) Remember, I had my binoculars, we were watching that couple getting undressed in the Pierre? They were on the eighth floor. I remember because we were looking for them the next night. We called them "The Couple on the Eighth Floor."

KAREN. I don't know what you called them, I called them "The Couple on the Seventh Floor." (*She walks away angrily into bedroom.*)

SAM. Look, it's pointless to argue about it. It's not important.

KAREN. (*From bedroom.*) If it's pointless then why are you pointing it out?

SAM. Because you made an issue of it.

KAREN. (*Crossing to bedroom door.*) Maybe I made an issue of saying we were in 719 but *you* made an issue of proving to me we *weren't* in 719.

SAM. All right, Karen. (*He walks away to fireplace.*)

KAREN. Don't tell me, "All right, Karen." If I thought it was 719, why didn't you have the decency to let me just go on in my ignorance and think it was 719?

SAM. Okay. Okay. I'm sorry. It was 719.

KAREN. Aw, forget it. It was 819. (*Moves back into bedroom.*)

SAM. (*Rushing into bedroom.*) No, no. As a matter of fact, you're right. I just remembered. It really was 719.

KAREN. I don't want it 719. I want it 819 . . . Look, why don't you go inside and lose some weight? (*That was a nasty remark.* SAM *glares at* KAREN, *then goes into living room, reassures himself with a glance at his waistline in the fireplace mirror, picks up work papers and sits.* KAREN *realizes what she's done. She crosses to living room*

and embraces him.) I'm sorry, Sam. (SAM *nods his head,
looks at his papers.* KAREN *moves around the sofa.*) We're
some lousy couple, aren't we? . . . Aren't we?

SAM. (*Doesn't look up.*) Mmm.

KAREN. Mmm what? (*Sitting on the arm of the sofa.*)

SAM. (*Looks up.*) Mmm, yes, we're some lousy couple.

KAREN. (*Without malice.*) That's what I said. First
thing we agreed on today.

SAM. Look, Karen, I really don't mean to be rude but
I *must* work on these estimates tonight. You understand.

KAREN. Sure, I understand.

SAM. I explained to you that Sid and Walter suddenly
came down with the flu—

KAREN. It's all right, Sam. You're excused . . . (*She
wanders aimlessly about the room. Catching sight of herself in the mirror over the chest, she examines her figure
and then decides to do some exercises, which she quickly
gives up. She sits on the arm of the sofa next to* SAM.) Do
you have any good estimates for me to read?

SAM. Isn't there anything to read in the bedroom?

KAREN. (*Shrugs.*) "Check-out time is three o'clock."
That's all I could find . . . Don't worry about me. I'll
find something to do.

(SAM *goes back to his papers.* KAREN *puts her arms
around his shoulders and rocks him playfully from
side to side, much to* SAM's *displeasure. Suddenly she
releases him, goes to the front door, opens it and goes
out into the hall.*)

SAM. What are you doing?

KAREN. (*Coming back into room.*) Looking for the
waiter.

SAM. Call him up.

KAREN. I thought I'd look in the hall first. Gives me
something to do. (*She goes back out into the hall.*) Nope,
don't see him. (*Comes back in and closes door.*) In five
minutes I'll call. See? I'll alternate them.

SAM. Karen, please.

KAREN. (*Crosses to him and takes his arm.*) Oh, come on. Forget your crummy old papers and take me to a dirty movie. (*Tries to pull him out of sofa.*) Come on, Sam. Let's go.

SAM. Stop it, Karen.

KAREN. You know what's playing on Sixth Avenue? "Cat House Confidential" and "Ursula the Slut." I passed it in the cab, I swear on my mother's life.

SAM. Don't be ridiculous.

KAREN. (*Kneeling by sofa.*) Are you afraid we'll be recognized? We'll buy beards in the Five and Ten.

SAM. If you want to go, go yourself. (*Trying to concentrate on papers.*)

KAREN. What happens if I get picked up?

SAM. Call me and I won't wait up for you.

KAREN. (*Hugging him.*) Oh, good, you've got your sense of humor back. All right, just take a walk with me. A ten-minute walk and I'll leave you alone.

SAM. Maybe later. We'll see.

KAREN. (*Getting up and pacing.*) No movies . . . no walk. (*She sits on top of the chest of drawers and picks up "What to Do in New York" magazine and skims through it. There is a silence. Finally:*) Feel like going back to the house and watching the paint dry? (SAM, *at the end of his patience, gets up with papers and moves into the bedroom.*) I'm just trying to think of something we can do together.

(*The DOORBELL rings.*)

SAM. (*Pacing in bedroom.*) Shall I get it or is that something you'd like for us to do together?

KAREN. Listen, I'll even take nastiness. It's not much but it's a start.

(KAREN *crosses to door and opens it. It's the* WAITER *with the food on a roller table. He is a middle-aged Puerto Rican.*)

WAITER. Good evening.

KAREN. (*Smiles.*) Hello.

WAITER. (*He rolls the table in.*) Would you like the table near the window?

KAREN. (*Moves towards bedroom.*) Sam, would you like the table near the window?

SAM. (*Disinterested.*) It doesn't make any difference.

KAREN. (*Sweetly, to* WAITER.) It doesn't make any difference.

WAITER. (*Leaving the table up near the windows.*) Shall I leave it here?

KAREN. Sam, should he leave it there?

SAM. (*Throwing contract on bed and moving to doorway.*) Here, there, anywhere, it doesn't make any difference.

KAREN. (*Shrugs, smiles at* WAITER.) Here, there, anywhere. It doesn't make any difference.

WAITER. (*Takes chair from desk and puts it to the right of the table.*) Yes, m'am. (*He gets armchair from right of sofa and brings it to the table.*)

SAM. (*To* WAITER.) You don't have to set up the chairs.

KAREN. (*To* WAITER.) You don't have to set up the chairs.

WAITER. Yes, m'am. (*He starts to put armchair back.*)

SAM. All right, leave them, you've done it already.

KAREN. Yes, why don't you just leave the chairs? They're all set up.

(WAITER *puts the chair back at table.*)

SAM. Can I have the bill, please?

WAITER. Yes, sir. (*Takes bill and pencil to* SAM.)

KAREN. (*She looks at tray of hors d'oeuvres on table. Sweetly.*) Oh, look at all the anchovies.

SAM. (*Signing bill.*) Didn't you tell them you didn't want anchovies?

WAITER. (*To* KAREN.) You didn't want anchovies?

KAREN. (*Doesn't want more trouble.*) No, no. I asked for anchovies. I'm a very big fan of anchovies.

SAM. (*Hands bill to* WAITER.) That'll be all, thank you.

KAREN. Yes, that'll be all, thank you.

WAITER. And thank you. (*Crosses to door.*)

KAREN. (*Looks at table.*) Wait a minute. The champagne. Where's the champagne?

WAITER. No champagne? (*Looks at check.*) You're right. They forgot the champagne.

KAREN. But the anchovies they remembered.

SAM. (*Returning to bedroom.*) I can't drink anything now, I've got work to do. What do you need a whole bottle of champagne for?

KAREN. It's our anniversary. (*To* WAITER.) It's our anniversary.

WAITER. Oh, congratulations.

KAREN. (*Sitting on arm of chair at table.*) Thank you. We're married twenty-three or twenty-four years today or tomorrow.

WAITER. Then you want the champagne?

KAREN. With two grown children in college.

WAITER. Oh? That's wonderful.

KAREN. (*Shrugs.*) You think so? He's flunking out and she's majoring in dirty clothes.

SAM. (*Greatly irritated, moves back to living room.*) He's not flunking out. Why do you say he's flunking out? (*Controls himself. To* WAITER.) That'll be all, thank you.

WAITER. If you don't want the champagne, I'll cross it off the bill.

SAM. She doesn't want the champagne. Cross it off the bill. (*Crosses back to bedroom.*)

KAREN. (*To* WAITER.) I *want* the champagne. Don't cross it off the bill. (*For* SAM's *benefit.*) Bring me a bottle and *one* glass.

WAITER. Yes, m'am.

SAM. (*From bedroom.*) That'll be all, thank you.

KAREN. Yes, that'll be all, thank you.

WAITER. (*Opening door.*) When you want me to take the table, just ring.

KAREN. (*Moving to* WAITER.) Yes, I'll ring when I want you to take the table.

WAITER. Thank you . . . And again, congratulations. (*He exits.*)

(SAM *crosses to table, takes cover off a dish.*)

KAREN. (*At mantel.*) Did you hear that, Sam? We're being congratulated on being married to each other.

SAM. (*Disgusted, slams cover back on dish.*) I asked for lean roast beef. That is not lean roast beef. (*Moves to sofa and sits, taking contract from coffee table.*)

KAREN. (*Contemplatively.*) You know how many people we know who are still married as long as us? One other couple. The Shelly's . . . The most boring people I ever met.

SAM. (*Cannot contain himself any more.*) Why do you talk to the waiter like that?

KAREN. Like what? (*Sits at table and begins to serve herself.*)

SAM. Like you've known him for twenty years. You just met him. He walked in here two minutes ago with fatty roast beef. It's none of his business how our son is doing in school.

KAREN. I was just having a conversation. I get lonely, I like to talk to people.

SAM. He's a waiter. Talk to him about food.

KAREN. I did something wrong again. I'm sorry, Sam. When he brings the champagne I'll hide behind the drapes.

SAM. You don't have to hide. Just don't tell him our personal problems, that's all.

KAREN. What should I do, lie?

SAM. Certainly, lie. Everybody else does. Tell them you have a beautiful and devoted daughter. Tell them you have a brilliant son who's on the Dean's list. Tell them you're only forty-two years old.

KAREN. There's no point to it. In two years I'll be fifty. Who's going to like me better if I'm only forty-two?

SAM. You don't have to revel in it like it's some kind of an accomplishment.

KAREN. I'm not insane about getting older. It happens to everyone. It's happened to you. You're fifty-one years old.

SAM. (*Nods his head in exasperation.*) That's the difference between us. I don't accept it. I don't have to accept being fifty-one. (*Getting up and moving to her.*) I don't accept getting older.

KAREN. Good luck to you. You'll be the youngest one in the cemetery.

SAM. We can't even have a normal discussion any more. (*He stalks into the bedroom, closes the door, and stretches out on the bed.*)

KAREN. Accept being fifty-one and I'll have a normal discussion. (*Stops as SAM closes door.*) Aren't you going to have your dinner? (*Gets up and examines the plate of meat. Holds up a piece to the bedroom door and calls to SAM.*) Sam, I found some very lean roast beef. (*She nibbles on a piece.*) Come inside and see how thin I'm getting. (*The DOORBELL rings.*) Hey, come on. The champagne is here. (*She opens door to bedroom and calls in.*) If you don't come out, I'll tell the waiter you wear dentures. (*She crosses and opens the front door.* JEAN McCORMACK *stands there. She is Sam's secretary. She is a trim, attractive woman about 28. She is neatly dressed, bright, cheerful and smilingly efficient.*) Oh! Hello, Miss McCormack.

JEAN. Hello, Mrs. Nash. I hope I'm not disturbing you.

KAREN. No, no, not at all. Mr. Nash and I were just sitting around, joking. Come in. (*Still holding roast beef in her hand.*)

JEAN. Thank you. (*She enters room, closing the door behind her.*) I hate to barge in this way but I have some papers that need Mr. Nash's signature immediately.

KAREN. Certainly. (*Calls out.*) Sam. It's Miss McCormack. (*To* JEAN.) It is *Miss* McCormack now, isn't it?

JEAN. (*Taking several contracts out of briefcase.*) It *was* Mrs. Colby last year. This year it's Miss McCormack again.

KAREN. (*Sitting on arm of sofa.*) Oh. You're lucky you can remember. I've been married so long if I got divorced, I'd have to make up a maiden name . . . Have you had your dinner yet? (*Indicates roast beef in her hand.*)

JEAN. (*Laying out contracts on coffee table front of sofa.*) I don't have dinner, thank you.

KAREN. No dinner? Ever?

JEAN. (*Getting glasses and pen from purse on console table behind sofa.*) I have a large breakfast, a moderate lunch and a snack before going to bed. On this job I've worked late so often, I had to readjust my eating routine. Now I'm used to it.

(SAM *gets up from bed and moves into living room.*)

KAREN. Oh. Well, I can understand that. I miss a lot of dinners with Mr. Nash too.

SAM. Oh, hello. You got them, huh? (*Sits on sofa and examines contract.*)

JEAN. Just came in. All ready for signature.

KAREN. (*To* JEAN.) How about some black coffee? Or would that fill you up?

JEAN. Black coffee would be fine, thank you.

KAREN. One black coffee coming up. Sam, would you like some black coffee?

SAM. No.

KAREN. That's no black coffee and one black coffee.

(KAREN *crosses to table,* SAM *is looking over the contracts.* MISS McCORMACK *sits next to him.* KAREN *pours coffee.*)

SAM. Why is there an adjustment on this figure?

JEAN. (*Looks at it.*) There was a clerical omission on the Cincinnati tabulations. It didn't show up on the 1400 but I rechecked it with my own files and made the correction. (*Points on respective pages of contract.*) So that item 17B should read three hundred and twenty-five thousand and disregard the figure on 17A.

KAREN. Cream and sugar?

JEAN. No, thank you.

SAM. But this should have been caught on the IBM.

JEAN. It should have but it wasn't. Obviously it wasn't fed properly.

KAREN. No cream and no sugar or no cream and yes, sugar?

JEAN. No cream and *no* sugar.

KAREN. So it's yes, no cream and no sugar.

SAM. Did you call this to Purcell's attention?

KAREN. (*Handing cup to* JEAN.) Would you like some pastry or cookies? I could call down. They have beautiful pastry and cookies here.

JEAN. This is fine, thank you. (*To* SAM.) Mr. Purcell says this happened once before this month. He can't pin it down until he rechecks the whole 66 file.

KAREN. (*Leaning on console table behind sofa.*) You're sure? A sandwich? A Welsh rarebit?

JEAN. No, I'm really quite happy, thank you. (*Takes saccharine from purse and puts it in coffee.*)

SAM. Well, I'm just going to have to go over this whole thing tonight with Howard. If we give Henderson any room for doubt, we can blow our entire presentation.

JEAN. (*Sips coffee.*) I told him there was a possibility of this so he made plans to stay in town tonight.

SAM. Damn! Of all nights to have this happen. (*Putting down contract.*) What time is it now?

JEAN. (*Looks at watch.*) Ten past five.

KAREN. (*Looking over* JEAN's *shoulder.*) Ten past five.

SAM. All right, you tell Howard I'll meet him in the office between six-fifteen and six-thirty. Tell him I want to see every one of last year's 1400 forms.

KAREN. (*Moving around sofa to* SAM.) You're going to the office? Tonight?

SAM. It can't be helped, Karen. (JEAN *puts coffee cup down.*) We're having that same damned trouble with the computer again.

KAREN. I could go with you. Maybe all it needs is a little dusting.

SAM. Something in that office sure as hell needs dusting. (*Getting up and moving to bedroom.* JEAN *gathers up the contracts and moves to put them in briefcase at the console table.*) All right, Miss McCormack, why don't you hop in a cab now and get started on these figures with Howard? I just want to clean up and I'll meet you in about twenty minutes.

JEAN. Yes, sir.

SAM. I hope I'm not ruining any plans you had for to-night?

JEAN. When I saw the figures this morning, I expected it. (*Closes case.* SAM *takes bottle of pills from attaché case and crosses to bathroom.*) Mrs. Nash, thank you very much for the coffee.

KAREN. You really should eat something. You'll faint right over the IBM machine.

JEAN. (*Opening front door.*) I'll be all right.

KAREN. (*Moving to her above sofa.*) It's a pity you can't stay two more minutes. I just ordered champagne. Can I tell her why, Sam?

SAM. (*Returns from bathroom, having taken pills. Throws pills back into case.*) What's that? (*Drinks from glass on dresser. Takes jacket from back of chair and puts it on.*)

KAREN. Well, I'm not supposed to go around blurting these things out but it's our twenty third anniversary . . .

JEAN. Oh? I didn't know. Congratulations.

KAREN. (*To* JEAN, *but for* SAM's *benefit.*) Thank you . . . Yes, life has been very good to me. I have a beautiful and devoted daughter, a brilliant son who's on the Dean's list, I'm forty-two years old, what more can I ask?

SAM. (*Moving into living room.*) Karen, Miss Mc-Cormack has to get back to the office. (SAM *goes back into bedroom, takes hair brushes from overnight bag and brushes hair in front of closet mirror.*)

KAREN. Oh, I'm sorry. (*To* JEAN.) Don't let him work you too late.

JEAN. It's all right. I'm used to it now. Best wishes again, Mrs. Nash.

KAREN. (*As* JEAN *starts out.*) Thanks, dear. And see that he buys me a nice gift.

JEAN. (*Smiles.*) I definitely will. (*Closes door.*)

KAREN. (*To* SAM.) What a sweet girl. That's a very sweet girl, Sam.

SAM. Karen, listen, I'm very sorry about tonight. It just can't be helped. (*Puts brushes back.*)

KAREN. That's a sweet, young, skinny girl.

SAM. (*Takes a cordless electric razor from attaché case and crosses to bathroom.*) The thing is, if I leave now maybe I can still get back in time for us to have a late dinner.

KAREN. (*Enters bedroom and sits in armchair.*) Oh, don't worry about me, Sam. (SAM *begins to shave.*) I understand. I just feel badly for you. You could have really relaxed tonight and instead you'll be cooped up in that stuffy office until all hours working over some boring contracts with your smooth shaven face.

SAM. (*Still shaving, moves into bedroom.*) Well, I can't very well walk through the lobby of the Plaza Hotel with a stubbly chin. (*Returns to bathroom.*)

KAREN. They wouldn't let you into the elevator. Don't forget your Jade East.

SAM'S VOICE. My what?

KAREN. Your sexy cologne. The doorman will never get you a cab if you don't smell nice.

SAM. (*Enters bedroom. Looks at* KAREN *for a moment and then shuts razor off.*) What are you doing, Karen?

KAREN. Oh, I'm just joking. Can't you tell when I'm kidding around any more, Sam?

SAM. No, I can't. (*Crosses around bed and puts razor back in case.*)

KAREN. (*Playfully pats his fanny, and then sits on bed.*) Well, of course I am. I'm just teasing you by intimating you're having an affair with your secretary.

SAM. I see. (*Takes overcoat from top of bureau and puts it on.*)

KAREN. Are you, Sam? Is sweet, skinny Miss McCormack your mistress?

SAM. For God's sakes, Karen, what kind of a thing is that to say?

KAREN. If you're not, it's a lousy thing to say. If you are, it's a hell of a question.

SAM. I'm not even going to dignify that with an answer.

KAREN. (*On her knees, bouncing up and down like a child.*) Oh, come on, Sam, dignify it. I'm dying to know. Just tell me if you're having an affair with her or not.

SAM. And you'll believe me?

KAREN. Of course.

SAM. No, I'm not having an affair with her.

KAREN. (*Big smile.*) Yes, you are.

SAM. Curses, trapped again. (*Looks out window.*) It looks like snow. I hope I can get a cab.

KAREN. (*Starting to take off hairpiece.*) Even if you're not, Sam, it's all right if you do. I approve of Miss McCormack. She's a nice girl.

SAM. (*Getting attaché case from bed.*) Thank you. She'll be pleased to know. Look, I could call downstairs and get you a ticket for a show tonight. There's no reason for you to sit alone like this. Is there something you'd like to see?

KAREN. (*Smiles.*) Yeah. What you and Miss McCormack will be doing later.

SAM. Really, Karen, I find this in very poor taste. (*Moving to living room, puts attaché case down on console table behind sofa.*)

KAREN. (*Getting brush from overnight case.*) Why? I'm just being honest again. I'm saying that if at this stage of your life you wanted to have a small, quiet affair with a young, skinny woman, I would understand. (*Sits back on bed and begins to brush out hairpiece.*)

SAM. (*Stops abruptly in his gathering of the contracts from coffee table and returns to bedroom.*) What do you mean at this stage of my life?

KAREN. (*Continues her brushing.*) Well, you're blankety years old. I would say the number but I know you don't accept it. And I realize that when a man becomes blankety-one or blankety-two, he is feeling insecure, that he's losing his virility, (*Smiles broadly at* SAM.) and that a quiet fling may be the best thing for him. I know, I read the New York Post.

SAM. I'm glad to know I have Rose Franzblau's permission.

KAREN. And mine if you really want it.

SAM. (*Yells.*) Well, I don't want it and *I'm not having an affair!*

KAREN. Then why are you yelling?

SAM. (*Crosses to living room.*) Because this is an idiotic conversation.

KAREN. (*Collapses on bed.*) Oh, Sam, I'm so glad.

SAM. (*Takes contracts from coffee table and puts them in case.*) Now you're happy? You're happy because *now* you don't think I'm having an affair?

KAREN. Well, of course I'm happy. You think I'm some kind of a domestic mental case? I don't want you having an affair. I'm just saying that if you *are* having one, I understand.

SAM. (*Crosses to bedroom, picks up contract from bed.*) Karen, I have a hard night's work ahead of me. I'll be back about twelve. (*Starts to leave.*)

KAREN. Sam, stay and talk to me for five minutes.

SAM. They're waiting for me at the office. I've got work to do.

KAREN. You've got help in the office. I've been with the firm longer than all of them . . . (*After a moment,* SAM *sits on the edge of the bureau.*) Sam, I know we haven't been very happy lately. I know you've been busy, you may not have noticed it, but we have definitely not been very happy.

SAM. Yes, Karen, I've noticed it.

KAREN. (*Continues to brush hairpiece.*) What's wrong? We have a twelve-room house in the country, two sweet children, a maid who doesn't drink, is there something we're missing?

SAM. I—don't know.

KAREN. Can you at least think about it? I need hints, Sam . . . (*Quoting.*) "Is there something else you want?" (SAM *doesn't answer.*) "Is there something I can give you that I'm not giving you?" (*Again no answer.*) Could you please speak up, we're closing in ten minutes.

SAM. It's me, Karen, it's not you. (*Crosses to living room, puts contract in case, closes it.*)

KAREN. (*Puts hair and brush on dresser and follows him into living room.*) I'll buy that. What's wrong with you, Sam?

SAM. (*There is a long pause.*) I don't know . . . (*Moves to mantel and then paces in front of sofa.*) I don't know if you can understand this . . . but when I came home after the war . . . I had my whole life in front of me. And all I dreamed about, all I wanted, was to get married, and to have children . . . and to make a success of my life . . . Well, I was very lucky . . . I got it all . . . Marriage, the children . . . more money than I ever dreamed of making . . .

KAREN. (*Sitting on sofa.*) Then what is it you want?

SAM. (*Stopping by fireplace.*) I just want to do it all over again . . . I would like to start the whole damned thing right from the beginning.

KAREN. (*Long pause.*) I see. Well, frankly, Sam, I don't think the Navy will take you again.

SAM. (*Smiles ruefully.*) Well, it won't be because I can't pass the physical. (*Takes case and starts for door again.*) I told you it's stupid talking about it. It'll work itself out. If not, I'll dye my hair. (*He opens the door.*)

KAREN. You know what I think? I think you want to get out and you don't know how to tell me.

SAM. (*Stops in door. Turns back to* KAREN.) That's not true.

KAREN. Which isn't? That you want to get out or that you don't know how to tell me?

SAM. Why do you always start the most serious discussions in our life when I'm halfway out the door?

KAREN. If that's what you want, just tell me straight out. Just say, "Karen, there's no point in going on." I'd rather hear it from you personally, than getting a message on our service.

SAM. Look, we'll talk about it when I get back, okay? (*He starts out again.*)

KAREN. (*Can no longer contain herself. There is none of that "playful, toying" attitude in her voice now. Jumping up.*) *No, God dammit, we'll talk about it now!* I'm not going to sit around a hotel room half the night waiting to hear how my life is going to come out . . . If you've got something to say, then have the decency to say it before you walk out that door.

(*There is a moment's silence while they try to compose themselves.* SAM *turns back into the room and closes the door.*)

SAM. Is there any coffee left?

KAREN. It's that bad, huh? . . . All right, sit down, I'll get you some coffee. (*She starts to cross to table and stops, looking at her hands.* SAM *crosses to sofa. Puts down attaché case by coffee table and sits.*) Look at this. I'm shaking like a leaf. Pour it yourself. I have a feeling in a few minutes I'm not going to be too crazy about you (KAREN *crosses and sits on ottoman next to sofa, hands clasped together.*)

SAM. (*He finds it difficult to look at her.*) No matter what, Karen, in twenty-three years my feelings for you **have never changed. You're my wife, I still love you.**

KAREN. Oh, God, am I in trouble.

SAM. It has nothing to do with you. It's something that just happened . . . It's true, I am having an affair with her . . . (SAM *waits for* KAREN *to react. She merely sits and looks at her hands.*) It's been going on for about six mon'hs now . . . I tried stopping it a few times, it didn't work . . . After a couple of days I'd start it again . . . And 'hen—well, what's the point in going on with this? You wanted honesty, I'm giving it to you. I'm having an affair with Jean, that's all there is to it.

KAREN. (*Looks up.*) Who's Jean?

SAM. Jean! Miss McCormack.

KAREN. Oh. For a minute I thought there were two of them.

SAM. I'm not very good at this. I don't know what I'm supposed to say now.

KAREN. Don't worry about it. You're doing fine. (*She gets up and moves to table.*) You want that coffee now? I just stopped shaking.

SAM. . . . What are we going to do?

KAREN. (*Turns back to* SAM.) Well, you're taken care of. You're having an affair. I'm the one who needs an activity.

SAM. Karen, I'll do whatever you want.

KAREN. Whatever *I* want?

SAM. I'll leave. I'll get out tonight . . . Or I'll stop seeing her. I'll get rid of her in the office. I'll try it any way you want.

KAREN. (*Moves to sofa.*) Oh. Okay. I choose "Stop Seeing Jean" . . . Gee, that was easy. (*Snaps her fingers.*) Now we can go back to our old normal life and li·e happily ever after. (*Starts to pour coffee, but stops and puts pot down.*) It's not my day. Even the coffee's cold.

SAM. Oh, come on, Karen, don't play "Aren't we civilized?" Call me a bas'ard. Throw the coffee at me.

KAREN. You're a bastard. You want cream and sugar?

SAM. It's funny how our attitudes have suddenly

changed. What happened to "I think a man of your age *should* have an affair"?

KAREN. It looked good in the window but terrible when I got it home.

SAM. If it's any solace to you, I never thought it would go this far. I don't even remember how it started . . .

KAREN. Think, it'll come back to you.

SAM. Do you know she worked for me for two years and I never batted an eye at her?

KAREN. Good for you, Sam.

SAM. (*Angry.*) Oh, come on. (*Crosses to bedroom, and stretches out across bed.*)

KAREN. (*She follows him into bedroom.*) No, Sam, I want to hear about it. She worked for you for two years and you didn't know her first name was Jean. And then one night you were both working late and suddenly you let down your hair and took off your glasses and she said, "Why, Mr. Nash, you're beautiful."

SAM. (*Takes pillow and places it over his head.*) That's it, word for word. You must have been hiding in the closet.

KAREN. (*Tears the pillow away and throws it back down on bed.*) All right, you want to know when I think the exact date your crummy little affair started? I'll tell you. It was June nineteenth. It was your birthday and you just turned fifty years old. Five oh, count 'em, folks, and you were feeling good and sorry for yourself. Right?

SAM. Oh, God, here comes Doctor Franzblau again.

KAREN. And the only reason you picked on Miss McCormack was because she was probably the first one you saw that morning . . . If she was sick that day, this affair very well could have been with your elevator operator.

SAM. Wrong. He's fifty-two and I don't go for older men.

KAREN. (*Breaks away and crosses to living room.*) You were right before, Sam. Let's discuss this later tonight.

SAM. (*Sitting up on side of bed.*) No, no. We've opened this up, let's bring it all out. I've told you the truth, I'm involved with another woman. I'm not proud of it, Karen, but those are the facts. Now what am I supposed to do about it?

KAREN. (*Moves back to bedroom doorway.*) Well, I *would* suggest committing suicide but I'm afraid you might think I meant *me* . . . (*Goes back to living room.*) I have one other suggestion. Forget it.

SAM. (*Sharply.*) Forget it?

KAREN. (*Pacing above sofa.*) I understand it, Sam. It's not your fault. But maybe I can live with it until it's over. What else can I do, Sam? I'm attached to you. So go out, have a good time tonight and when you come home, bring me the Daily News, I'm getting sick of the Post. (*Sits on sofa.*)

SAM. If I lived with you another twenty-three years, I don't think I'd ever understand you.

KAREN. If that's a proposition, I accept.

SAM. (*Gets up and moves to* KAREN.) Dammit, Karen, stop accepting everything in life that's thrown at you. Fight back once in a while. Don't understand me. Hate me! I am *not* going through a middle-aged adjustment. I'm having an affair. A cheating, sneaking, sordid affair.

KAREN. If it helps you to romanticize it, Sam, all right. I happen to know better.

SAM. (*Crossing above sofa to fireplace.*) You don't know better at all. You didn't even know I was having an affair.

KAREN. I suspected it. You were working three nights a week and we weren't getting any richer.

SAM. (*Leaning on mantlepiece.*) I see. And now that you know the truth I have your blessings.

KAREN. No, just my permission. I'm your wife, not your mother.

SAM. That's indecent. I never heard such a thing in my life. For crying out loud, Karen, I'm losing all respect for you.

KAREN. What's the matter, Sam, am I robbing you of

all those delicious guilt feelings? Will you feel better if I go to pieces and try to lash back at you?

SAM. (*Crosses below sofa.*) At least I would unders'and it. It's normal. I don't know why you're not having hysterics and screaming for a lawyer.

KAREN. (*Getting up to confront him.*) All right, Sam, if it'll make you happier . . . I think you stink. You're a vain, self-pi'ying, deceiving, ten-pound box of rancid no-Cal cottage cheese. How'm I doing?

SAM. Swell. Now we're finally getting somewhere.

KAREN. Oh, you like this, don't you? It makes everything nice and simple for you. Now you can leave here the martyred, misunderstood husband. Well, I won't give you the satisfaction. I take it back, Sam. (*Sits on sofa. Pleasantly, with great control.*) You're a pussycat. I'll have milk and cookies for you when you get home.

SAM. (*Sits on ottoman.*) No, no. Finish what you were saying. Get it off your chest, Karen. It's been building up for twenty-three years. I want to hear everything. Vain, self-pitying, what else? Go on, what else?

KAREN. You're adorable. Eat your heart out.

SAM. (*Furious.*) Karen, don't do this to me.

KAREN. I'm sorry, I'm a forgiving woman. I can't help myself.

SAM. (*Gets up, takes case and crosses to door.*) You're driving me right out of here, you know that, don't you?

KAREN. There'll always be room for you in my garage.

SAM. If I walk out this door now, I don't come back.

KAREN. I think you will.

SAM. What makes you so sure?

KAREN. You forgot to take your eye drops.

SAM. (*He storms to coffee table, snatches up drops and crosses back to door. Stops.*) Before I go I just want to say one thing. Whatever you think of me is probably true. No, not probably, *definitely*. I have been a bas'ard right from the beginning. I don't expect you to forgive me.

KAREN. But I do.

SAM. (*Whirling back to her.*) Let me finish. I don't expect you to forgive me. But I ask you with all conscience, with all your understanding, not to blame Jean for any of this.

KAREN. (*Collapses on couch. Then pulling herself together.*) I'll send her a nice gift.

SAM. (*Puts down case beside sofa.*) She's been torturing herself ever since this started. *I'm* the one who forced the issue.

KAREN. (*Moving away from him on sofa, mimics* JEAN.) "It didn't show up on the 1400 but I rechecked it with my own files and made the correction on the 640." . . . You know as well as I do that's code for "I'll meet you at the Picadilly Hotel."

SAM. (*Kneeling beside sofa.*) You won't believe me, will you? That she's a nice girl.

KAREN. Nice for you and nice for me are two different things.

SAM. If it's that Sunday supplement psychology you're using, Karen, it's backfiring because you're just making it easier for me.

KAREN. Well, you like things easy, don't you? You don't even have an affair the hard way.

SAM. Meaning what?

KAREN. (*Getting up.*) Meaning you could have at least taken the trouble to look outside your office for a girl . . . (*Picks up imaginary phone.*) "Miss McCormack, would you please come inside and take an affair!" . . . Honestly, Sam. (*Moves above sofa.*)

SAM. Karen, don't force me to say nice things about her to you.

KAREN. I can't help it. I'm just disappointed in you. It's so damned unoriginal.

SAM. What did you want her to be, a fighter pilot with the Israeli Air Force?

KAREN. *Everyone* cheats with their secretary. I expected more from *my* husband!

SAM. (*Shaking his head.*) I never saw you like this.

You live with a person your whole life, you don't really know them.

KAREN. (*Crossing below sofa to bedroom.*) Go on, Sam, go have your affair. You're fifty-one years old. In an hour it may be too late. (*Sits at dresser, and brushes hair.*)

SAM. (*Getting up and crossing to her in bedroom.*) By God, you are something. You are really something special, Karen. Twenty-three years I'm married to you and I still can't make you out. You don't look much different than the ordinary woman but I promise you there is nothing walking around on two legs that compares in any way, shape or form to the likes of you.

KAREN. (*Drops brush and turns to him. Laughing.*) So if I'm so special, what are you carrying on with secretaries for?

SAM. I'll be God-damned if I know . . .

(*They look at each other. He turns and starts to front door, taking attaché case.*)

KAREN. (*Following him into living room.*) Sam! (SAM *stops.*) Sam . . . do I still have my two choices? (*He turns and looks at her.*) Because if I do . . . I choose "Get rid of Miss McCormack." (*He looks away.*) I pick "Stay here and work it out with me, Sam." (KAREN *turns her back to him and leans against the arm of the sofa.*) Because the other way I think I'm going to lose. Don't go to the office tonight, Sam . . . Stay with me . . . Please.

SAM. (*Leaning on console table, looks at her.*) I swear, I wish we could go back the way it was before. A couple of years ago, before there were any problems

KAREN. Maybe we can, Sam. We'll do what you said before. We'll lie. We'll tell each other everything is all right . . . There is nothing wrong in the office tonight, there is no Miss McCormack and I'm twenty-seven God-damned years old . . . What do you say, Sam?

SAM. (*Moves about indecisively.*) Maybe tomorrow, Karen . . . I can't—tonight! (*He opens door.*) I'll— I'll see you.

KAREN. When? (*He exits, leaving door open.*) Never mind. I love surprises.

(*As* SAM *leaves, the* WAITER *appears with a tray with an ice bucket filled with a bottle of champagne and two glasses.*)

WAITER. The champagne . . . I brought two glasses just in case. (*He closes the door and places the ice bucket and glasses on the desk. He glances back.*) Is he coming back?

KAREN. (*Remains leaning on sofa.*) Funny you should ask that.

(*He begins to open the bottle.*)

CURTAIN

VISITOR FROM HOLLYWOOD

CAST

WAITER
JESSE KIPLINGER
MURIEL TATE

ACT TWO

SCENE: *Suite 719 at the Plaza.*

TIME: *About three in the afternoon on a warm, sunny, spring day.*

AT RISE: *The WAITER is just finishing setting up some fresh glasses and bottles of liquor on top of the bureau between the windows in the living room. The TELEPHONE in the bedroom rings. JESSE KIPLINGER emerges from the bathroom. JESSE is about 40, a confident, self-assured man. He is applying after shave lotion to his face. He is dressed in "Hollywood Mod," with a tan turtleneck sweater and tight blue suede pants. His shoes are highly polished and buckled. He has the latest-style haircut, with bangs falling over his forehead. He crosses to the phone and picks it up.*

JESSE. Hello? . . . Oh, just a minute. (*He drops phone and crosses to the* WAITER.) I'll take that. (*He indicates the check, which the* WAITER *hands him. He signs it and returns it to the* WAITER, *who nods and crosses to the door.* JESSE *picks up the phone and holds his hand over the phone until the* WAITER *is gone, closing the door behind him. Then into phone.*) Put her on . . . (*Waits, then in a much softer, romantically persuasive tone.*) Hello? . . . Muriel? Where are you? . . . Well, come on up . . . Yes, I'm positive it's all right . . . (*More insistently.*) Muriel, do you want me to come down and get you? . . . All right then, take the elevator and come to suite 719 . . . And stop being so silly, I'm dying to see you. (*He hangs up. Thinks a second, then picks up phone again.*) Hello, operator? This is Mr. Kiplinger in suite

47

719. Would you please hold all local calls for the next hour, I'm going to be in conference . . . (*Checks appointment book on night table.*) Make that an hour and a half . . . Thank you. (*He hangs up and begins to clear the bed of a collection of scripts, trade papers, and galley proofs. Kneeling, he pushes them under the bed. Rising, he carefully smooths the spread. He snatches up a section of colored comics from the arm of the armchair and throws it into the waste basket. Taking a blue button-down sweater from the back of chair at dresser, he puts it on with a great flair and carefully examines himself in the mirror on the closet door. Satisfied with his appearance, he crosses to living room and checks the bar set-up on the bureau. The front DOORBELL rings.* JESSE *crosses to answer it, checking his hair in the mirror over the mantle as he does. He is finally ready. Taking a deep breath, he opens the door.* MURIEL TATE *stands there.* MURIEL *is in her late thirties and is extremely attractive. She wears a bright yellow spring coat and a simple, demure, high-necked grey dress which shows off her svelte, still girlish figure. Her hair falls simply to her shoulders, held back by a wide, white band.* MURIEL *is a warm, easy-smiling woman who seems as naïve and vulnerable as the day she graduated from Tenafly High School. When the door opens, the* TWO *of them greet each other with enormous smiles.* JESSE *throws out his arms.*) Muriel!

MURIEL. (*Smiles, cocks her head.*) Jesse?

JESSE. It's not.

MURIEL. It is.

JESSE. Muriel, I can't believe it. Is it really you?

MURIEL. It's me, Muriel.

JESSE. Well, come on in, for pete's sakes, come on in.

MURIEL. (*Enters with a rush and crosses below sofa to far side of sofa.*) I can only stay for a few minutes.

JESSE. (*Closes door, follows to below near side of sofa.*) My God, it's good to see you.

(*They stand and confront each other.*)

MURIEL. I just dropped in to say hello. I really can't stay.

JESSE. You sounded good on the phone but you look even better.

MURIEL. Because I've got to get back to New Jersey. I'm parked in a one-hour zone. Hello, Jesse, I think I'm very nervous.

JESSE. Hey! Hello, Muriel.

MURIEL. Same old Muriel, heh?

JESSE. What do you mean, same old Muriel? You look fantastic. (*Arms outstretched, moves to her.*) Come here, let me take a good look at you.

MURIEL. (*Evading him, crosses below coffee table.*) Oh, don't, Jesse. Don't look at me. I've been stuck in the Holland Tunnel for two hours. What time is it? Tell me when it's three o'clock. I can't stay. (*Sits in armchair.*)

JESSE. (*Moves towards her.*) Muriel, I can't get over it. You look absolutely wonderful.

MURIEL. Well, I *feel* absolutely wonderful.

JESSE. (*Sitting on arm of sofa.*) I really, sincerely mean that. You simply look incredibly fantastic.

MURIEL. Well, I *feel* incredibly fantastic.

JESSE. Well, you look it.

MURIEL. Well, I *feel* it.

JESSE. And how are you?

MURIEL. (*Without enthusiasm.*) I'm all right . . . I don't know why I'm so nervous, do you? (*Shrugging coat off shoulders, and arranging it over back of chair.*)

JESSE. No. I can't imagine why you should be so nervous.

MURIEL. Neither can I. I just am . . . Should I be here?

JESSE. Why not? Is there anything wrong in it?

MURIEL. Oh, no. No, of course not. There's nothing wrong in it. My God, no. I don't see anything wrong. I just dropped by from New Jersey to say hello. What's wrong with that? . . . I just don't think I should be here.

(*Getting up, and moving towards mantel.*) Is it three o'clock yet?

JESSE. (*Moving towards her.*) Little Muriel Tate, all grown up and married. How many kids you got now?

MURIEL. Three.

JESSE. No kidding? Three kids . . . What are they?

MURIEL. A boy and a girl.

JESSE. A boy and a girl?

MURIEL. (*Breaking away to other side of sofa.*) And another boy who's away in camp. I can't even think straight. Isn't this terrible?

JESSE. (*Moving to sofa. Good-naturedly.*) What's wrong?

MURIEL. I don't know, I can't catch my breath. Well, it's *you*, that's the simple explanation. I'm nervous about meeting you.

JESSE. Me? Me? Jesse Kiplinger, your high-school boy friend from Tenafly, New Jersey. Ohh, Muriel.

MURIEL. You know what I mean, Mr. "Famous Hollywood Producer" staying at the Plaza Hotel.

JESSE. Mr. Famous Hollywood Producer. (*Sitting on sofa.*) Muriel, you know me better than that. I haven't changed. I made a couple of pictures, that's all.

MURIEL. (*Moving to sofa.*) A couple of pictures? The Easter show at the Radio City Music Hall? I stood on line with my children for three hours in the rain.

JESSE. What did you do that for? You could have called my office in New York. My girl would have gotten you right in. Any time you want to see one of my pictures—

MURIEL. Oh, I couldn't do that.

JESSE. Why not?

MURIEL. I couldn't. I couldn't impose like that.

JESSE. You're *not* imposing.

MURIEL. I am.

JESSE. I *want* you to.

MURIEL. What's the number?

JESSE. I'll give it to you before you go. (*Getting up.*)

But first you're going to sit down and have a drink.
There's a million things I'm dying to ask you.

MURIEL. Oh, no drinks for me.

JESSE. One little drink.

MURIEL. No, no, no. You go ahead and have a drink.
I have a five o'clock hairdresser's appointment.

JESSE. You don't drink?

MURIEL. Oh, once in a great, great while. Anyway, I've
got to get home. I shouldn't even be in the city. The kids
will be home from school soon and I've got to make dinner
for Larry and I haven't even done my shopping in Bonwit's. No, no, I just dropped by to say hello.

JESSE. What'll you have?

MURIEL. A Vodka stinger.

JESSE. Coming right up. (*He crosses to the bar set-up.*)

MURIEL. (*Sitting on sofa.*) And then I've got to go . . .
Whoooo, I finally took a breath. That felt good.

JESSE. (*Pouring liquor into shaker.*) Will you relax?
Will you, Muriel? Come on now. I want you to stop being
so silly and relax.

MURIEL. (*Chiding.*) Is that how you talk to your stars
when they're nervous? Is that what you say to Elke
Sommer?

JESSE. I don't talk to the stars. I have directors for
that . . . For God's sakes, Muriel, what are you so nervous about?

MURIEL. Oooh, there's that famous Hollywood temper
I read about . . . You want me to be frank?

JESSE. Please.

MURIEL. I feel funny sitting here drinking in a hotel
room . . . I mean, I'm a married woman.

JESSE. (*Having finished making and pouring drinks,
moves to her.*) Would you feel better if we had our drinks
down in the Palm Court?

MURIEL. We're here, we might as well stay.

JESSE. (*Handing her drink.*) Okay. Then will you sit
back and relax? (*Sits down next to her on sofa.*)

MURIEL. Just for a few minutes. I've got a six o'clock hairdresser's appointment.

JESSE. I thought it was at five?

MURIEL. It's flexible . . . Is it warm in here? (*Putting down drink on coffee table.*)

JESSE. Why don't you take off your gloves?

MURIEL. (*Shaking finger at him.*) Oh, no . . . ! Let's not have any of *that,* Mr. Jesse Kiplinger of Hollywood, California . . . My gloves will stay where they belong, if you please.

JESSE. (*Putting drink down on coffee table.*) Muriel, you are delightfully and incredibly unchanged. How long has it been now? Fifteen, sixteen years?

MURIEL. Since our last date? It'll be seventeen years on August sixth.

JESSE. You remembered that?

MURIEL. I still have the swizzle sticks from Tavern on the Green.

JESSE. (*Leaning in to her.*) No, time hasn't changed you, Muriel. You're still so fresh and clean. (*Sniffs about her.*) You even smell the same way.

MURIEL. Ohhh?

JESSE. (*Sniffs her ear.*) Like cool peppermint . . . Clear, cool peppermint.

MURIEL. (*Pushes his nose away with her finger.*) Now, you and your nose just behave yourself . . . I did not come to the Plaza Hotel to be smelled.

JESSE. And now you've blossomed and matured . . . only in reverse . . . You look younger and fresher and . . . well, you know what I mean. I just think you look absolutely fantastic.

MURIEL. (*Pulls herself together. Clears her throat. Very businesslike.*) You going to be in New York long, Jesse?

JESSE. Possibly just till the weekend. I've got to sign a director for my new picture.

MURIEL. John Huston?

JESSE. Yes. How did you know that?

MURIEL. Oh, we keep up on things in Tenafly . . . Mr. Famous Hollywood Producer, staying at the Plaza Hotel signing up John Huston for his next picture. (*Playfully pushing his leg.*)

JESSE. I might stay over another few days. It depends . . . on what develops.

(*He looks down at leg. She gets up nervously.*)

MURIEL. I've never been in the Plaza before. It's beautiful. (*Stops near door to bedroom, which is opened.*) What's in there?

JESSE. The bedroom. You can go in.

MURIEL. (*Shying away, moves back to sofa.*) It's all right, I take your word for it . . . Is this where you meet with John Huston? I mean does he sit in here and the two of you talk and then he signs the contract? Is that how you do it?

JESSE. (*Lolling back on sofa.*) In this very room . . . Will you stop with the celebrity routine. Aside from a couple of extra pounds, I'm still the same boy who ran anchor on the Tenafly track team.

MURIEL. And is living in the old Humphrey Bogart house in Beverly Hills.

JESSE. How did you know that?

MURIEL. (*Moving to ottoman.*) Never mind, I know, I know . . . Maybe I haven't seen you in seventeen years, but I know an awful lot about you, Mr. Jesse Kiplinger . . . (*Sits.*) *Pootch!*

JESSE. Pootch?

MURIEL. Isn't that what they call you in Hollywood? Your nickname? Pootch?

JESSE. *G*ootch!

MURIEL. I thought it was Pootch.

JESSE. No. No, no, it's Gootch.

MURIEL. I thought I read that you have all your shirts specially made by Pucci in Florence, so they call you **Pootch.**

JESSE. No, no. I have all my shoes made by *G*ucci in Rome so they call me Gootch.

MURIEL. Oh.

JESSE. (*Deprecatingly.*) It's a silly thing. I don't know why they print stories like that.

MURIEL. Because people like me like to read them. Are those Gucci shoes you're wearing now, Gootch?

JESSE. These? (*To display shoes, puts one foot up on coffee table, the other over the arm of the sofa.*) No. These are the one pair I had made in England. You can't get this leather in Italy. No, I have a man in Bond Street makes them for me . . . MacCombs.

(MURIEL *reacts to the sight of his wide-spread legs and turns away in embarrassment.*)

MURIEL. (*Attempting to make a joke.*) Well, they're beautiful shoes, Mac*Cootch!*

JESSE. MacCootch! That's very good. (*He laughs.*) Hey, can we stop talking about me for a while?

MURIEL. (*Turns back to him.*) Why? I think you're very interesting to talk about.

JESSE. Well, I don't. I'm very bored with me. I'm much more interested in you . . . (*Sits up and hands her drink.*) But first let's have our drinks.

MURIEL. And then I've got to go. (*Takes glass.*)

JESSE. Let's say, to renewing old acquaintances.

MURIEL. You drink to that. (*Moves to sofa.*) I'll drink to your new picture winning the Academy Award.

JESSE. Muriel, it's not going to win the Academy Award. It's not even going to get nominated. (*Beginning to laugh.*) As a matter of fact, it's a piece of crap . . . (*Catches himself.*) Excuse me, Muriel.

MURIEL. (*Sitting on sofa.*) Be that as it may, it's going to gross over nine million. Domestic.

JESSE. That's beside the point . . . How did you know that?

MURIEL. I know, I know, Mr. "Gootch" Kiplinger . . . I've been following your career very closely, if you please.

JESSE. (*Moving closer.*) Muriel, it is so exciting seeing you again. The minute you walked in that door, I got a— a tingle, all over, the way I used to . . . You know what I mean.

MURIEL. (*Trying to remain matter-of-fact.*) I'm sure I don't. I have three children and I'm very happy and I have a wonderful life and I have no business being in a hotel room in New York at three o'clock in the afternoon with a man I haven't seen since Tavern on the Green seventeen years ago— (*He kisses her on the lips. She looks at him.*) Any particular reason you did that?

JESSE. (*Still leaning towards her.*) I wanted to. Desperately.

MURIEL. Do you always blithely go ahead and do whatever you want to?

JESSE. If I can get away with it . . . As a matter of fact . . . if you don't object too strenuously, I'm going to kiss you again.

MURIEL. And then I've got to go. (JESSE *kisses her again tenderly on the lips. Lets him kiss her for a moment. Then jumps up and moves away.*) Woo . . . That'll be enough of that, Mr. Do-Whatever-You-Want-To Kiplinger. Wow, that Vodka stinger has really gone to my head.

JESSE. (*Noncommittally.*) It's even better when you drink it.

MURIEL. (*Takes drink from coffee table and crosses to chair.*) Now, don't confuse me. I'm nervous enough as it is. Cheers. (*Drinks.*) Was it good?

JESSE. (*Taking drink.*) What? The drink?

MURIEL. The kiss.

JESSE. The kiss? Yes, the kiss was very good.

MURIEL. What did it feel like?

JESSE. What do you mean, what did it feel like?

MURIEL. (*Sitting in chair.*) Was it a good kiss or a

medium kiss or a waste-of-time kiss? I'm interested in knowing your reaction.

JESSE. Why? You never asked me that when I kissed you in Tenafly.

MURIEL. You weren't a famous Hollywood producer living in Humphrey Bogart's house signing John Huston for your next picture in Tenafly. Can I please have your reaction to my kiss?

JESSE. It was a superb kiss.

MURIEL. (*Puts drink down on floor next to chair. Takes compact from purse on chair.*) It wasn't superb. I don't kiss superbly. It was an average, inexperienced, everyday New Jersey kiss . . . I don't know why I let you kiss me anyway, "Mr. Famous Hollywood Kisser." (*Powdering face.*)

JESSE. (*Smiles warmly.*) Is it possible that you are the last, sweet, simple, unchanged, unspoiled woman living in the world today?

MURIEL. I'm sure I don't know what you're talking about. (*Looking in compact mirror.*) Oh, God, look at my lips. I'd never get past the house detective. What time is it?

JESSE. (*Looks at watch.*) Twenty after.

MURIEL. Three? Already? I've got to go. (*Puts compact back in purse, gets up and begins to gather purse and coat from chair.*)

JESSE. Not yet.

MURIEL. I must.

JESSE. Ten more minutes?

MURIEL. I can't . . .

JESSE. Please!

MURIEL. I'll stay five. (*Sits back down in chair.*)

JESSE. Good.

MURIEL. . . . Why did you call me yesterday?

JESSE. (*Smiles.*) I called you because, believe it or not, I've been thinking about you.

MURIEL. For seventeen years?

JESSE. On and off.

MURIEL. In Humphrey Bogart's old house? I don't believe you, "Mr. International Liar." And I don't trust you. (*She gets up and again begins to gather her belongings.*) And I'm not staying.

JESSE. (*Quietly.*) Goodbye.

MURIEL. (*Stops in surprise.*) Do you mean that?

JESSE. I don't want to force you to stay here. You know what's best for you.

MURIEL. (*Looks at him.*) I'll just finish my drink. (*She puts her things back on the chair and picks up her drink.*)

JESSE. Muriel, you must believe me when I tell you I ha.e no ulterior motives in asking you here today. I just wanted to see you. I'm trying to impress you with the fact that you are the only, solitary, real, honest-to-goodness, unphony woman that I have been with since the day I arrived in Hollywood seventeen years ago.

MURIEL. What about your mother?

JESSE. She's the worst one.

MURIEL. (*Sitting next to him on sofa.*) Well, your mother must be very proud to have such a famous son.

JESSE. (*Edges closer to her.*) Do you know, in my own quiet way, I was crazy about you?

MURIEL. (*Puts drink down on table.*) As a matter of fact, everyone in Tenafly is proud of you. Even Larry, my husband, talks about you all the time. He always says, "Jesse Kiplinger, Jesse Kiplinger, that's all I ever hear around this house." (*Stops and thinks about what she has just said.*)

JESSE. I remember exactly what you looked like the day I left for California. You were wearing a tan raincoat, a tweed skirt and a brown sweater. And a little locket that your grandmother had given you. (*Traces locket on her chest.*) Do you remember?

MURIEL. I remember when your first picture came to Tenafly, that's what I remember. Everybody went. Do you know it was the only Jeff Chandler picture that ever played two weeks at the Hillside Drive-In?

JESSE. Even then, you had a quality about you, Muriel,

that was sort of—well, untouched. (*Puts hand on outside of her leg and caresses her.*) You were the only girl that gave me pleasure in just holding her hand.

MURIEL. (*Determinedly ignoring* JESSE'S *actions.*) You know, a lot of the girls from school still kid me about you. I mean when they see your name in a column or something like that.

JESSE. I didn't expect to see it any more, Muriel, that quality of honesty . . . and frankness . . . that ability to cut through deceit (*Moves hand and going underneath her skirt, puts it between her legs.*) and phoniness with just one look through those big, unsuspecting, wide-open eyes. I really did not expect to see it again in my lifetime.

MURIEL. They always kid me and say, "Oh, if I married you instead of Larry, I'd be living in Hollywood now, going to parties with James Garner and Otto Preminger, running around with the Rat Pack."

JESSE. You don't know what you are. You really don't . . . Well, I'll tell you what you are. You're something very special. I *know*, Muriel.

MURIEL. . . . I mean I wouldn't even know what to say to Otto Preminger.

JESSE. Don't change, Muriel. Don't ever change the sweet, simple way you are.

(*He kisses her neck, deeply. For a minute she is lost in the embrace and then, without changing her mood:*)

MURIEL. Do you know Frank Sinatra?

JESSE. (*Slowly comes out of her neck and looks at her.*) Who?

MURIEL. Frank Sinatra. Did you ever meet him?

JESSE. (*Slightly shaken, pulls back, takes his hand away and sits back on sofa.*) Yes. Yes, I know Frank.

MURIEL. What's he like?

JESSE. Frank? . . . I . . . I don't really know him that well, we had dinner a few times.

MURIEL. Where? In his house?

JESSE. Once in a restaurant, once I think in his house. I don't remember.

MURIEL. Was Mia there?

JESSE. Uh . . . no. This was before he met Mia.

MURIEL. So in other words, you never met Mia?

JESSE. Yes, I did meet Mia but she wasn't married to Frank then.

MURIEL. I see. They say he's very generous. Is that true? Is he as generous as they say?

JESSE. Yeah, I guess so. He served very large portions . . . I don't know. Christ, who cares about Frank Sinatra?

MURIEL. (*Hurt.*) I'm sorry—I was just curious. I didn't mean to pry into your personal life. Well, I've got to be going. (*She gets up and moves to chair.*)

JESSE. (*Apologetic.*) Wait, Muriel . . .

MURIEL. (*Getting belongings from chair.*) No, I've got to leave before the traffic starts. If I get stuck in the Holland Tunnel again and I'm late for Larry's dinner, he'll want to know where I was and I don't lie very well and oh, God, I don't know why I came here in the first place . . . (*Drops things back in chair. Becoming more and more upset.*) What have I done?

JESSE. You haven't done anything, Muriel.

MURIEL. (*Pacing.*) Haven't done anything? I'm sitting there letting you kiss me and smell me . . .

JESSE. Muriel, if I've done anything to offend you, I'm sorry.

MURIEL. (*Moving towards windows.*) I must have been out of my mind, coming to the Plaza Hotel in the middle of the week.

JESSE. There is no reason to get yourself upset. I didn't do anything worse than give you a friendly kiss.

MURIEL. (*Coming back to sofa.*) I happen to enjoy a wonderful reputation.

JESSE. I'm glad you enjoy it . . . Now stop being so silly. Sit down and finish your drink.

MURIEL. I suppose you'll go back to Hollywood and have a big laugh with Otto Preminger over this.

JESSE. I wouldn't dream of it.

MURIEL. Promise.

JESSE. I promise.

MURIEL. Say it. Say, "I will not have a big laugh with Otto Preminger over this."

JESSE. I don't even *talk* to Otto Preminger. Why would I laugh at you? I have nothing but respect and the warmest of feelings for you.

MURIEL. You do? God's truth?

JESSE. God's truth. You're an angel.

MURIEL. Really . . . ? (*She hesitates a moment. Sits on the arm of the sofa.*) Would I fit in with your crowd?

JESSE. No, you would not fit in with my crowd. You're too good for them. You're too sweet and honest for the whole slimy bunch.

MURIEL. . . . But which ones would I fit in with?

JESSE. Muriel, I don't know what kind of distorted image you have of these people, but they're not what you think they are. *I'm* not what you think I am. All these things you read in the paper about me being witty, charming, the boy genius, that's only part of the story. Do you know what kind of a life I really lead in Hollywood?

MURIEL. Are you going to tell me?

JESSE. Yes, I'll tell you. Why did I call you yesterday? After seventeen years? Okay, let's start with, "Yes, I'm a Famous Hollywood Producer. Yes, I never made a picture that lost money. Yes, I got that magic touch, call it talent, whatever you want, I don't know." . . . The fact is, ever since I was old enough to sneak into the Ridgewood Theatre in Tenafly, I've been a movie nut. (*Getting up, stands by sofa.*) Not only have I seen every Humphrey Bogart movie he ever made at least eight times. I now own a print of all those pictures. Why do you think I was so crazy to buy his house? (*Moves slowly to window.*) So I went to Hollywood and was very lucky and extremely smart and presto, I became a producer. (*Unobtrusively pulls down the shade.*) I love making movies. Some are good, some are bad, most of them are fun. I hope I can continue doing it for the next fifty years. That's one half of my life. The other half is that in the last fourteen years I've been married three times—to three of the worst bitches you'd ever want to meet. (*Gets bottle of Vodka and glass from bar.*)

MURIEL. Jesse, you don't have to tell me any of this if you don't want to.

JESSE. Maybe you're right. (*Moves to front door and locks it.*) Maybe I shouldn't be telling you about my sordid Hollywood past. (*Leans on mantle.*)

MURIEL. (*Settling down on the sofa, picks up her drink.*) So you married these three bitches, then what happened?

JESSE. (*Moves to* MURIEL.) What happened . . . I gave them love, I gave them a home, I gave them a beautiful way of life—and the three bitches took me for every cent I got. (*Refills her glass, then sits on floor by arm-chair.*) But I don't even care about the money, screw it—excuse me, Muriel. What hurts is that they took the guts out of me.—They were phony, unfaithful, all of them. Did you know I caught my first wife, Dolores, in bed with a jockey? A jockey! (*Indicates size, holding hand a foot off the floor.*) Do you know what it does to a man's self-respect to find his wife in the sack with a four-foot-eight shrimp, weighs a hundred and twelve pounds? . . . But as I said before, screw it. Tell me if I'm shocking you, Muriel. (*Refills his own drink.*)

MURIEL. I'll let you know. (*Drinks.*)

JESSE. All right . . . My second wife, Carlotta . . . She was *keeping* her Spanish guitar teacher . . . *Keeping him!* . . . I never caught her but she didn't fool me. *No one* takes twenty-seven thousand dollars worth of guitar lessons in one year . . .

MURIEL. Is Carlotta the one you met at Kirk Douglas's house?

JESSE. Yes, as a matter of fact. Was that in the paper too?

MURIEL. Sheilah Graham's column. It was a big party for the Ukrainian Folk Dancers and the Los Angeles Rams.

JESSE. (*Getting up, replenishes her drink.*) Muriel, forget the Los Angeles Rams . . . (*Putting bottle and his glass down on the console table, he crosses behind sofa.*) Listen to what I'm saying to you. I am in a very bad way. I've been through three hellish, miserable marriages. I don't want to go that route again. I am losing my faith and belief that there is anything left that resembles an uncorrupt woman . . . (*Sighs.*) So last week my mother, who still gets the Tenafly newspaper, shows me a picture of the PTA annual outing at Palisades this year and who is there on the front page, coming in first in the Mother and Daughter Potato Race, (*Leans in to* MURIEL *over side arm of couch.*) looking every bit as young and lovely and as sweet as she did seventeen years ago, was my last salvation . . . Muriel Tate. (*Gradually moving to bedroom door.*) That's why I had to see you, Muriel. Just to talk to you, to have a drink, to spend five minutes, to reaffirm my faith that there *are* decent women in this world . . . even if it's only one . . . even if you're the last of a dying species . . . if somebody like you exits, Muriel . . . then maybe there's still somebody for me . . . *That's* why I called you yesterday. (JESSE *has finished his speech. He is somewhat spent, emotionally. He moves to the bed and sits.*)

MURIEL. (*Getting up and moving toward bedroom door.*) Well . . . well . . . well . . .

JESSE. (*From the bedroom.*) I hope whatever I said didn't embarrass you, Muriel . . . but hell, if you expect honesty from another person you can't be anything less than honest yourself.

MURIEL. (*Still at doorway.*) I'm not embarrassed, I'm flattered. To think a famous person like you wants to confide in a plain person like me . . .

JESSE. (*Gets up and moves to her in living room.*) Now

you finish your Vodka stinger and then I'm going to let you go.

MURIEL. (*Pouring herself drink at bar.*) Oh, I've got plenty of time. Larry's never home till seven. (*She holds up drink.*) Cheers.

(*She drinks.* JESSE *crosses to* MURIEL, *touches her.*)

JESSE. How are you, Muriel? Are you happy?

MURIEL. Happy? . . . Oh, yes. I think if I'm anything, I'm happy. (*Moves down to sofa.*)

JESSE. I'm glad. You deserve happiness, Muriel.

MURIEL. Yes, Larry and I are very happy . . . (*She drinks.*) I would have to say that Larry and I have one of the happier marriages in Tenafly. (*She drinks again.*)

JESSE. That's wonderful.

MURIEL. I mean we've had our ups and downs like any married couple but I think in the final analysis what's left is . . . that we're happy.

JESSE. (*Moves down to her.*) I couldn't be more pleased. Well, listen, it's no surprise. Larry's a wonderful guy.

MURIEL. Do you think so?

JESSE. Don't you?

MURIEL. Yes, *I* do. But no one else seems to care for him. (*Sits on sofa.*) Of course, they don't know him the way *I* do. I'm out of stinger again. (*Holds glass out to* JESSE.)

JESSE. (*Takes her glass.*) Are you sure you're going to be all right? I mean driving?

MURIEL. (*Gradually feeling the effects of the drinks, she slowly exposes a whole, new, unexpected* MURIEL.) If I had to worry about getting home every time I had three Vodka stingers, I'd give up driving. (JESSE *crosses to bar, looking back at her in puzzlement.*) Yes, I'd say that in spite of everything, Larry and I have worked out happiness . . . or some form of it.

JESSE. Is he doing well in business? (*Fills her glass once again.*)

MURIEL. Oh, in business you don't have to worry. In that department he's doing great. I mean he's really got a wonderful business there . . . Of course, it was good when my father had it. (JESSE *hands her drink.*) Ooh, cheers. (*She drinks.*)

JESSE. (*Sitting on arm of sofa.*) In what department isn't he doing well?

MURIEL. He's doing well in *every* department.

JESSE. Are you sure?

MURIEL. I'm positive.

JESSE. Then I'm glad.

MURIEL. Why, what do you hear?

JESSE. I haven't heard a thing except what you're telling me.

MURIEL. Well, I'm telling you that we have a happy marriage. Are you trying to infer, we don't have a happy marriage?

JESSE. No . . .

MURIEL. Well, you're wrong. We have a happy marriage. A God-damned happy marriage. (*Tries to put glass down on table, misses and nearly slips off the sofa.*) Oh, I'm sorry. I should have had lunch.

JESSE. (*Steadies her and picks up glass from floor and puts it on table.*) Shall I order down for some food?

MURIEL. No, I can't stay. Larry'll be home about five.

JESSE. I thought he comes home at seven.

MURIEL. If he comes home at all . . . Please forgive me, Jesse, I seem to be losing control of myself.

JESSE. You drank those too quickly. Didn't you have anything to eat all day?

MURIEL. Just an olive with the two stingers I had downstairs . . . I'll be all right.

JESSE. Do you want to lie down for a while?

MURIEL. What's the point? You're going back to Hollywood in a few days . . . Oh, I see what you mean . . . Oh, God, I'm sorry, Jesse, I seem to be running off at the mouth.

JESSE. (*Sits down next to her.*) What is it, Muriel? What's with you and Larry?

MURIEL. Nothing. I told you, we're very happy. We have tiny, little differences like every normal couple but basically we're enormously happy together. I couldn't ask for a better life . . . (*And she throws her arms around* JESSE *and gives him a full, passionate kiss on the lips, then she pulls away.*) Oh, you shouldn't have done that, Jesse. I'm very vulnerable right now and you mustn't take advantage . . . I'm going. I've got to go. (*Gets up and moves away.*)

JESSE. (*Taking her hand.*) Muriel, I didn't know.

MURIEL. (*Pulling away.*) No, Jesse, don't.

JESSE. Why didn't you let me know?

MURIEL. (*Crying, crosses to chair for her things.*) Who knew you were interested? You were always at a party with the Los Angeles Rams.

JESSE. I never suspected for a minute. Why didn't you write to me?

MURIEL. (*Crying.*) Where? I don't know where Humphrey Bogart lived. (*Rushes to* JESSE *where he sits on sofa, and throws her arms about him.*) I've got to go. Let me go.

JESSE. (*With his arms about her waist.*) God, how I thought about you on the plane all the way to New York.

MURIEL. Please, Jesse. I've got to buy something in Bonwit's and get dinner for Larry. (*He munches on her neck.*) Don't bite my neck, it'll leave marks.

JESSE. You're different, Muriel. I know you are. You're not like any of the others. (*Caressing her.*)

MURIEL. I'm not different, Jesse. I'm a woman. A happily married woman with normal desires and passions. Please don't rub me. (*Pulls away from him.*)

JESSE. (*Reaching out for her.*) My life is empty, Muriel. Empty. But you can fill it for me. You can. (*Gets up and moves to her.*)

MURIEL. (*Retreating behind chair.*) I can't fill your life for you, Jesse, I've got to get home. Larry'll kill me.

JESSE. (*Catching her hands.*) Stay! An hour. Just one hour, that's all.

MURIEL. No, no. Tomorrow I'll be alone with my regrets and you'll be out there with Dino and Groucho . . .

JESSE. (*Pulling her above sofa in the direction of the bedroom.*) One hour, Muriel. Live my life with me for one hour.

MURIEL. No, please, Jesse. I've got to pick up my lamb chops.

JESSE. One hour, Muriel. The world can change for one hour.

MURIEL. (*Stopping above sofa.*) Can it, Jesse? Can it really?

JESSE. (*Moving behind her.*) It can for me, Muriel. It can for you.

MURIEL. I don't know, Jesse. I just don't know.

JESSE. All right, we'll just talk. (*Reaches around her waist from behind her, and places his hand on her stomach. Soothingly.*) No one ever got hurt just talking, did they?

MURIEL. . . . I suppose not.

JESSE. Of course they didn't. (*Rubbing her stomach.*)

MURIEL. (*Under the spell of his soft voice.*) What'll we talk about?

JESSE. Whatever you say. Whatever you want.

MURIEL. . . . Did you go to the Academy Awards dinner last year?

JESSE. (*Resignedly.*) Certainly. I go every year.

MURIEL. Oh, God, really?

JESSE. Really.

(*For a moment, they rock gently back and forth, but slowly, almost as in a dance step, he leads her into the bedroom.*)

MURIEL. Who did you sit next to?

JESSE. (*As if to a child.*) In the theatre, I sat next to Steve McQueen on one side and Liza Minelli on the other.

MURIEL. She's adorable, isn't she?

(*They move into bedroom.*)

JESSE. A real pixie.

MURIEL. And who did you sit with at the dinner?

JESSE. (*Leading her to bed.*) Well, let's see, at my table there was Charlton Heston and his wife, Joseph E. Levine, the producer, Eva Marie Saint, Marge and Gower Champion . . . (*Sits down on side of the bed.*)

MURIEL. Oh, they're cute . . . All at your table?

JESSE. (*Drawing her down on his knee.*) All at my table. And at the next table—there was Anthony Quinn and Virna Lisi, Paul Newman and Joanne . . . (*Searches for name.*)

MURIEL. Woodward . . .

JESSE. Woodward . . . (*He begins to unzip her dress.*) And there was Dean Jones and Yvette Mimieux . . .

MURIEL. Together . . . ?

JESSE. Yes, together . . . (*He gently forces her back down on the bed, at the same time pulling the dress off her shoulders.*) Then behind us there was Troy Donahue and Stella Stevens, Sammy Davis, Jr. and Margot Fonteyn . . .

(*They are both lying on the bed. The LIGHTS have faded out.*)

CURTAIN

VISITOR FROM FOREST HILLS

CAST

Norma Hubley
Roy Hubley
Borden Eisler
Mimsey Hubley

ACT THREE

SCENE: *Suite 719 at the Plaza.*

TIME: *Three o'clock on a warm Saturday afternoon in Spring.*

AT RISE: *The living room is bedecked with vases and baskets of flowers. In the bedroom one opened valise rests on the floor, containing a young woman's street clothes. A very large box, which had held a wedding dress, rests on the luggage rack, and a man's suit lies on the bed. A fur wrap and gloves are thrown over the back of the sofa. Telegrams of congratulation and newspapers are strewn about. The suite today is being used more or less as a dressing room since a wedding is about to occur downstairs in one of the reception rooms. As we come up,* NORMA HUBLEY *is at the phone in the bedroom, impatiently tapping the receiver. She is dressed in a formal cocktail dress and a large hat, looking her very best as any woman would want to on her daughter's wedding day. But she is extremely nervous and harassed, and with good cause as we'll soon find out.*

NORMA. (*On phone.*) Hello? . . . Hello, operator? . . . Can I have the Blue Room, please . . . The Blue Room . . . Is there a Pink Room? . . . I want the Hubley-Eisler wedding . . . The Green Room, that's it. Thank you . . . Could you please hurry, operator, it's an emergency . . . (*She looks over at the bathroom nervously. She paces back and forth.*) Hello? . . . Who's this? . . . Mr. Eisler . . . It's Norma Hubley . . . No, everything's fine . . . Yes, we're coming right down . . . (*She is smiling and trying to act as pleasant and as calm as*

71

possible.) Yes, you're right, it certainly *is* the big day
. . . Mr. Eisler, is my husband there? . . . Would you,
please? . . . Oh! Well, I'd like to wish you the very best
of luck too . . . Borden's a wonderful boy . . . Well,
they're *both* wonderful kids . . . No, no. She's as calm as
a cucumber . . . That's the younger generation, I guess
. . . Yes, everything seems to be going along beautifully
. . . Absolutely beautifully . . . Oh, thank you. (*Her
husband has obviously just come on the other end because
the expression on her face changes violently and she
screams a rasping whisper filled with doom. Sitting on
bed.*) Roy? You'd better get up here right away, we're in
big trouble . . . Don't ask questions, just get up here
. . . I hope you're not drunk because I can't handle this
alone . . . Don't say anything. Just smile and walk lei-
surely out the door . . . and then get the hell up here as
fast as you can. (*She hangs up, putting the phone back
on night table. She crosses to the bathroom and then puts
her head up against the door. Aloud through bathroom
door.*) All right, Mimsey, your father's on his way up.
Now, I want you to come out of that bathroom and get
married. (*There is no answer.*) Do you hear me? . . . I've
had enough of this nonsense . . . Unlock that door!
(*That's about the end of her authority. She wilts and almost pleads.*) Mimsey, darling, please come downstairs
and get married, you know your father's temper . . . I
know what you're going through now, sweetheart, you're
just nervous . . . Everyone goes through that on their
wedding day . . . It's going to be all right, darling. You
love Borden and he loves you. You're both going to have
a wonderful future. So please come out of the bathroom!
(*She listens, there is no answer.*) Mimsey, if you don't
care about your life, think about mine. Your father'll kill
me. (*The front DOORBELL rings.* NORMA *looks off nervously and moves to the other side of the bed.*) Oh, God,
he's here! . . . Mimsey! Mimsey, please, spare me this
. . . If you want, I'll have it annulled next week, but
please come out and get married! (*There is no answer*

from the bathroom but the front DOORBELL rings impatiently.) All right, I'm letting your father in. And heaven help the three of us!

(*She crosses through the bedroom into the living room. She crosses to the door and opens it as* ROY HUBLEY *bursts into the room.* ROY *is dressed in striped trousers, black tail coat, the works. He looks elegant but he's not too happy in this attire. He is a volatile, explosive man equipped to handle the rigors of the competitive business world, but a nervous, frightened man when it comes to the business of marrying off your only daughter.*)

ROY. What are you standing here? There are sixty-eight people down there drinking my liquor. If there's gonna be a wedding, let's have a wedding. Come on! (*He starts back out the door but sees that* NORMA *is not going anywhere. She sits on the sofa. He comes back in.*) Didn't you hear what I said? There's another couple waiting to use the Green Room. Come on, let's go! (*He makes a start out again.*)

NORMA. (*Very calm.*) Roy, could you sit down a minute? I want to talk to you about something.

ROY. (*She must be mad.*) You want to talk *now?* You had twenty-one years to talk while she was growing up. I'll talk to you when they're in Bermuda. Can we please have a wedding?

NORMA. We can't have a wedding until you and I have a talk.

ROY. Are you crazy? While you and I are talking here, there are four musicians playing downstairs for seventy dollars an hour. I'll talk to you later when we're dancing. Come on, get Mimsey and let's go. (*He starts out again.*)

NORMA. That's what I want to talk to you about.

ROY. (*Comes back.*) Mimsey?

NORMA. Sit down. You're not going to like this.

ROY. Is she sick?

Norma. She's not sick . . . exactly.

Roy. What do you mean, she's not sick exactly? Either she's sick or she's not sick. Is she sick?

Norma. She's not sick.

Roy. Then, let's have a wedding! (*He crosses into bedroom.*) Mimsey, there's two hundred dollars worth of cocktail frankfurters getting cold downstairs . . . (*He looks around empty room.*) Mimsey? (*He crosses back to living room to the side of the sofa. He looks at* Norma.) Where's Mimsey?

Norma. Promise you're not going to blame me.

Roy. Blame you for what? What did you do?

Norma. I didn't do anything. But I don't want to get blamed for it.

Roy. What's going on here? Are you going to tell me where Mimsey is?

Norma. Are you going to take an oath you're not going to blame me?

Roy. *I take it! I take it!* NOW WHERE THE HELL IS SHE?

Norma. . . . She's locked herself in the bathroom. She's not coming out and she's not getting married.

Roy. (*He looks at* Norma *incredulously. Then, because it must be an insane joke, he smiles at her. There is even the faint glint of a chuckle. Softly.*) . . . No kidding, where is she?

Norma. (*Turns away.*) He doesn't believe me. I'll kill myself.

Roy. (*He turns and storms into the bedroom. He crosses to the bathroom and knocks on the door. Then he tries it. It's locked. He tries again. He bangs on the door with his fist.*) Mimsey? . . . *Mimsey?* . . . *MIMSEY?* (*There is no reply. Girding himself, he crosses back through bedroom into living room to the sofa. He glares at* Norma.) All right, what did you say to her?

Norma. (*Jumping up and moving away.*) I knew it! I knew you'd blame me. You took an oath. God'll punish you.

Roy. I'm not blaming you. I just want to know what *stupid* thing you said to her that made her do this.

Norma. I didn't say a word. I was put ing on my lips ick, she was in the bathroom, I heard the door go click, it was locked, my whole life was over, what do you want from me?

Roy. And you didn't say a word?

Norma. Nothing.

Roy. (*Ominously moving towards her as* Norma *backs away.*) I see. In other words, you're trying to tell me that a normal, healthy, in'elligent twenty-one-year-old college graduate, who has driven me crazy the last eighteen months with wedding lists, floral arrangemen's and choices of assorted hors. d'oeuvres, has suddenly decided to spend this, the most important day of her life, locked in the Plaza Hotel john?

Norma. (*Making her stand at the mantle.*) Yes! Yes! Yes! Yes! Yes!

Roy. (*Vi ious.*) YOU MUSTA SAID SOMETHING! (*He storms into the bedroom.*)

Norma. (*She goes after him.*) Roy . . . Roy . . . What are you going to do?

Roy. (*Stopping below bed.*) First I'm getting the college graduate out of the bathroom! Then we're gonna have a wedding and then you and I are gonna have a big talk! (*He crosses to bathroom door and pounds on it.*) Mimsey! This is your father. I want you and your four-hundred-dollar wedding dress out of there in five seconds!

Norma. (*Standing at side of bed.*) Don't threaten her. She'll never come out if you threaten her.

Roy. (*To* Norma.) I got sixty-eight guests, nine waiters, four musicians and a boy with a wedding license waiting downstairs. This is no time to be diplomatic. (*Bangs on door.*) Mimsey! . . . Are you coming out or do we have the wedding in the bathroom?

Norma. Will you lower your voice! Everyone will hear us.

Roy. (*To* Norma.) How long you think we can keep

this a secret? As soon as that boy says "I do" and there's no one standing next to him, they're going to suspect something. (*He bangs on door.*) You can't stay in there forever, Mimsey. We only have the room until six o'clock . . . *YOU HEAR ME?*

(*There is still no reply from the bathroom.*)

NORMA. Roy, will you please try to control yourself?

ROY. (*With great display of patience, moves to foot of bed and sits.*) All right, I'll stay here and control myself. You go downstairs and marry the short, skinny kid. (*Exploding.*) *What's the matter with you?* Don't you realize what's happening?

NORMA. (*Moving to him.*) Yes. I realize what's happening. Our daughter is nervous, frightened and scared to death.

ROY. Of what? OF WHAT? She's been screaming for two years if he doesn't ask her to marry him, she'll throw herself off the Guggenheim Museum . . . What is she scared of?

NORMA. I don't know. Maybe she's had second thoughts about the whole thing.

ROY. (*Getting up and moving to bathroom door.*) Second thoughts? This is no time to be having *second thoughts.* It's costing me eight thousand dollars for the *first* thoughts. (*He bangs on door.*) Mimsey, open this door.

NORMA. Is that all you care about? What it's costing you? Aren't you concerned about your daughter's happiness?

ROY. (*Moving back to her below bed.*) Yes! Yes, I'm concerned about my daughter's happiness. I'm also concerned about that boy waiting downstairs. A decent, respectable, intelligent young man . . . who I hope one day is going to teach that daughter of mine to grow up.

NORMA. You haven't the faintest idea of what's going through her mind right now.

ROY. Do you?

NORMA. It could be anything. I don't know, maybe she thinks she's not good enough for him.

ROY. (*Looks at her incredulously.*) Why? What is he? Some kind of Greek God? He's a plain kid, nothing . . . That's ridiculous. (*Moves back to door and bangs on it.*) Mimsey! Mimsey, open this door. (*He turns to* NORMA.) Maybe she's not in there.

NORMA. She's in there. (*Clutches her chest and sits on side of bed.*) Oh, God, I think I'm having a heart attack.

ROY. (*Listening at door.*) I don't hear a peep out of her. Is there a window in there? Maybe she tried something crazy.

NORMA. (*Turning to him.*) That's right. Tell a woman who's having a heart attack that her daughter jumped out the window.

ROY. Take a look through the keyhole. I want to make sure she's in there.

NORMA. She's in there, I tell you. Look at this, my hand keeps bouncing off my chest. (*It does.*)

ROY. Are you gonna look in there and see if she's all right or am I gonna call the house detective?

NORMA. (*Getting up and moving below bed.*) Why don't *you* look?

ROY. Maybe she's taking a bath.

NORMA. Two minutes before her own wedding?

ROY. (*Crossing to her.*) What wedding? She just called it off.

NORMA. Wouldn't I have heard the water running?

ROY. (*Making a swipe at her hat.*) With that hat you couldn't hear Niagara Falls! . . . Are you going to look to see what your daughter's doing in the bathroom or do I ask a stranger?

NORMA. (*Crossing to door.*) I'll look! I'll look! I'll look! (*Reluctantly she gets down on one knee and looks through keyhole with one eye.*) Oh, my God!

ROY. What's the matter?

NORMA. (*To him.*) I ripped my stockings. (*Getting up and examining stocking.*)

ROY. Is she in there?

NORMA. She's in there! She's in there! (*Hobbling to far side of bed, and sitting down on edge.*) Where am I going to get another pair of stockings now? How am I going to go to the wedding with torn stockings?

ROY. (*Crossing to bathroom.*) If *she* doesn't show up, who's going to look at *you?* (*He kneels at door, looks through keyhole.*) There she is. Sitting there and crying.

NORMA. I *told* you she was in there . . . The only one in my family to have a daughter married in the Plaza and I have torn stockings.

ROY. (*He is on his knees, his eye to the keyhole.*) Mimsey, I can see you . . . Do you hear me? . . . Don't turn away from me when I'm talking to you.

NORMA. Maybe I could run across to Bergdorf's. They have nice stockings. (*Crosses to purse on bureau in bedroom, and looks through it.*)

ROY. (*Still through keyhole.*) Do you want me to break down the door, Mimsey, is that what you want? Because that's what I'm doing if you're not out of there in five seconds . . . Stop crying on your dress. Use the towel!

NORMA. (*Crossing to ROY at door.*) I don't have any money. Give me four dollars, I'll be back in ten minutes.

ROY. (*Gets up and moves below bed.*) In ten minutes she'll be a married woman because I've had enough of this nonsense. (*Yells in.*) All right, Mimsey, stand in the shower because I'm breaking down the door.

NORMA. (*Getting in front of door.*) Roy, don't get crazy.

ROY. (*Preparing himself for run at door.*) Get out of my way.

NORMA. Roy, she'll come out. Just talk nicely to her.

ROY. (*Waving her away.*) We already had nice talking. Now we're gonna have door breaking. (*Through door.*) All right, Mimsey, I'm coming in!

NORMA. No, Roy, don't! Don't!

(*She gets out of the way as* ROY *hurls his body, led by*

his shoulder with full force against the door. It doesn't budge. He stays against door silently a second, he doesn't react. Then he says calmly and softly:)

Roy. Get a doctor.

Norma. *(Standing below door.)* I knew it. I knew it.

Roy. *(Drawing back from door.)* Don't tell me I knew it, just get a doctor. *(Through door.)* I'm not coming in, Mimsey, because my arm is broken.

Norma. Let me see it. Can you move your fingers? *(Moves to him and examines his fingers.)*

Roy. *(Through door.)* Are you happy now? Your mother has torn stockings and your father has a broken arm. How much longer is this gonna go on?

Norma. *(Moving Roy's fingers.)* It's not broken, you can move your fingers. Give me four dollars with your other hand, I have to get stockings. *(Starts to go into his pockets. He slaps her hands away.)*

Roy. Are you crazy moving a broken arm?

Norma. Two dollars, I'll get a cheap pair.

Roy. *(As though she were a lunatic.)* I'm not carrying any cash today. Rented, everything is rented.

Norma. I can't rent stockings. Don't you even have a charge-plate? *(Starts to go through his pockets again.)*

Roy. *Slaps her hands away. Then pointing dramatically.)* Wait in the Green Room! You're no use to me here, go wait in the Green Room!

Norma. With torn stockings?

Roy. Stand behind the rented potted plant. *(Takes her by the arm and leads her below bed. Confidentially.)* They're going to call from downstairs any second asking where the bride is. And *I'm* the one who's going to have to speak to them. *Me! Me! ME! (The PHONE rings. Pushing her toward phone.)* That's them. *You* speak to them!

Norma. What happened to *me me me?*

(The PHONE rings again.)

Roy. (*Moving to bathroom door.*) Answer it. Answer it.

(*The PHONE rings again.*)

Norma. (*Moving to phone.*) What am I going to say to them?

Roy. I don't know. Maybe something'll come to you as you're talking.

Norma. (*Picks phone up.*) Hello? . . . Oh, Mr. Eisler . . . Yes, it certainly is the big moment. (*She forces a merry laugh.*)

Roy. Stall 'em. Stall 'em. Just keep stalling him. Whatever you do, stall 'em! (*Turns to door.*)

Norma. (*On phone.*) Yes, we'll be down in two minutes. (*Hangs up.*)

Roy. (*Turns back to her.*) Are you *crazy?* What did you say that for? I told you to stall him.

Norma. I stalled him. You got two minutes. What do you want from me?

Roy. (*Shakes arm at her.*) You always panic. The minute there's a little crisis, you always go to pieces and panic.

Norma. (*Shaking her arm back at him.*) Don't wave your broken arm at me. Why don't you use it to get your daughter out of the bathroom?

Roy. (*Very angry, kneeling to her on bed.*) I could say something to you now.

Norma. (*Confronting him, kneels in turn on bed.*) Then why don't you say it?

Roy. Because it would lead to a fight. And I don't want to spoil this day for you. (*He gets up and crosses back to bathroom door.*) Mimsey, this is your father speaking . . . I think you know I'm not a violent man. I can be stern and strict, but I have never once been violent. Except when I'm angry. And I am really angry now, Mimsey. You can ask your mother. (*Moves away so* Norma *can get to door.*)

Norma. (*Crossing to the bathroom door.*) Mimsey, this

is your mother speaking. It's true, darling, your father is very angry.

Roy. (*Moving back to door.*) This is your father again, Mimsey. If you have a problem you want to discuss, unlock the door and we'll discuss it. I'm not going to ask you this again, Mimsey. I've reached the end of my patience. I'm gonna count to three . . . and by God, I'm warning you, young lady, by the time I've reached three . . . *this door better be open!* (*Moving away to below bed.*) All right— One! . . . Two! . . . THREE! (*There is no reply or movement from behind the door. Roy helplessly sinks down on the foot of the bed.*) Where did we fail her?

Norma. (*Crosses to far side of bed, consoling him as she goes, and sits on edge.*) We didn't fail her.

Roy. They're playing "Here Comes the Bride" downstairs and she's barricaded in a toilet, we must have failed her.

Norma. (*Sighs.*) All right, if it makes you any happier, we failed her.

Roy. You work and you dream and you hope and you save your whole life for this day, and in one click of a door, suddenly everything crumbles. Why? What's the answer?

Norma. It's not your fault, Roy. Stop blaming yourself.

Roy. I'm not blaming myself. I know *I've* done my best.

Norma. (*Turns and looks at him.*) What does that mean?

Roy. It means we're not perfect. We make mistakes, we're only human. I've done my best and we failed her.

Norma. Meaning *I* didn't do my best?

Roy. (*Turning to her.*) I didn't say that. I don't know what your best is. Only *you* know what your best is. Did you do your best?

Norma. Yes, I did my best.

Roy. And I did my best.

NORMA. Then we *both* did our best.

ROY. So it's not our fault.

NORMA. That's what I said before.

(*They turn away from each other. Then:*)

ROY. (*Softly.*) Unless one of us didn't do our best.

NORMA. (*Jumping up and moving away.*) I don't want to discuss it any more.

ROY. All right, then what are we going to do?

NORMA. I'm having a heart attack, *you* come up with something.

ROY. How? All right, I'll go down and tell them. (*Gets up and moves to bedroom door.*)

NORMA. (*Moving to door in front of him.*) Tell them? Tell them what?

(*As they move into the living room, she stops him above the sofa.*)

ROY. I don't know. Those people down there deserve some kind of an explanation. They got all dressed up, didn't they?

NORMA. What are you going to say? You're going to tell them that my daughter is not going to marry their son and that she's locked herself in the bathroom?

ROY. What do you want me to do, start off with two good jokes? They're going to find out *some* time, aren't they?

NORMA. (*With great determination.*) I'll tell you what you're going to do. If she's not out of there in five minutes, we're going to go out the back door and move to Seattle, Washington! . . . You don't think I'll be able to show my face in this city again, do you? (ROY *ponders this for a moment. Then reassures her with a pat on the arm. Slowly he turns and moves into the bedroom. Suddenly, he loses control and lets his anger get the best of him. He grabs up the chair from the dresser, and bran-*

*dishing it above his head, he dashes for the bathroom
door, not even detouring around the bed but rather crossing right over it. Screaming and chasing after him.)* ROY!

(At the bathroom door, ROY *manages to stop himself in
time from smashing the chair against the door, trem-
bling with frustration and anger. Finally, exhausted,
he puts the chair down below the door and straddles
it, sitting leaning on the back.* NORMA *sinks into the
bedroom armchair.)*

ROY. Would you believe it, last night I cried. Oh, yes.
I turned my head into the pillow and lay there in the
dark, crying, because today I was losing my little girl.
Some stranger was coming and taking my little Mimsey
away from me . . . so I turned my back to you—and
cried . . . Wait'll you hear what goes on *tonight!*

NORMA. *(Lost in her own misery.)* I should have in-
vited your cousin Lillie. *(Gestures to the heavens.)* She
wished this on me, I know it. *(Suddenly* ROY *begins to
chuckle.* NORMA *looks at him. He chuckles louder, although there is clearly no joy in his laughter.)* Do you
find something funny about this?

ROY. Yes, I find something funny about this. I find it
funny that I hired a photographer for three hundred
dollars. I find it hysterical that the wedding pictures are
going to be you and me in front of a locked bathroom!
(Gets up and puts chair aside.) All right, I'm through
sitting around waiting for that door to open. *(He crosses
to bedroom window and tries to open it.)*

NORMA. *(Following after him.)* What are you doing?

ROY. What do you think I'm doing? *(Finding it im-
possible to open it, he crosses to living room and opens a
window there. The curtains begin to blow in the breeze.)*

NORMA. *(Crosses after him.)* If you're jumping, I'm
going with you. You're not leaving *me* here alone.

ROY. *(Looking out window.)* I'm gonna crawl out along
that ledge and get in through the bathroom window. *(He
starts to climb out window.)*

NORMA. Are you crazy? It's seven stories up. You'll kill yourself. (*She grabs hold of him.*)

ROY. It's four steps, that's all. It's no problem, I'm telling you. Now will you let go of me.

NORMA. (*Struggling to keep him from getting out window.*) Roy, no! Don't do this. We'll leave her in the bathroom. Let the hotel worry about her. Don't go out on the ledge. (*In desperation, she grabs hold of one of the tails of his coat.*)

ROY. (*Half out the window, trying to get out as she holds onto his coat.*) You're gonna rip my coat. Let go or you're gonna rip my coat. (*As he tries to pull away from her, his coat rips completely up the back, right up to the collar. He stops and slowly comes back into the room. NORMA has frozen in misery by the bedroom door after letting go of the coat. ROY draws himself up with great dignity and control. He slowly turns and moves into the bedroom, stopping by the bed. With great patience, he calls toward the bathroom.*) Hey, you in there . . . Are you happy now? Your mother's got torn stockings and your father's got a rented ripped coat. Some wedding it's gonna be. (*Exploding, he crosses back to the open window in the living room.*) Get out of my way!

NORMA. (*Puts hand to her head.*) I'm getting dizzy. I think I'm going to pass out.

ROY. (*Getting her out of the way.*) You can pass out *after* the wedding . . . (*He goes out window and onto the ledge.*) Call room service. I want a double Scotch the minute I get back.

(*And he disappears from view as he moves across the ledge. NORMA runs into the bedroom and catches a glimpse of him as he passes the bedroom window, but then he disappears once more.*)

NORMA. (*Bemoaning her fate.*) He'll kill himself. He'll fall and kill himself, that's the way my luck's been going all day. (*She staggers away from the window and leans on the bureau.*) I'm not going to look. I'll just wait until I hear a scream. (*The TELEPHONE rings and* NORMA *screams in fright.*) Aggghhh!! . . . I thought it was him . . . (*She crosses to the phone by the bed. The TELE- PHONE rings again.*) Oh, God, what am I going to say? (*She picks it up.*) Hello? . . . Oh, Mr. Eisler. Yes, we're coming . . . My husband's getting Mimsey now . . . We'll be right down. Have some more hors d'oeuvres . . . Oh, thank you. It certainly *is* the happiest day of my life. (*She hangs up.*) No, I'm going to tell him I've got a hus- band dangling over Fifty-ninth Street. (*As she crosses back to the opened window, a sudden torrent of RAIN begins to fall. As she gets to the window and sees it.*) I knew it! I knew it! It had to happen . . . (*She gets closer to the window and tries to look out.*) Are you all right, Roy? . . . Roy? (*There's no answer.*) He's not all right, he fell. (*She staggers into the bedroom.*) He fell, he fell, he fell, he fell . . . He's dead, I know it. (*She col- lapses onto the armchair.*) He's laying there in a puddle in front of Trader Vic's . . . I'm passing out. This time I'm really passing out! (*And she passes out on the chair, legs and arms spread-eagled. The DOORBELL rings, she jumps right up.*) I'm coming! I'm coming! Help me, who- ever you are, help me! (*She rushes through bedroom into living room and to the front door.*) Oh, please, somebody, help me, please!

(*She opens the front door and* ROY *stands there dripping wet, fuming, exhausted and with clothes disheveled and his hair mussed.*)

ROY. (*Staggering into room and weakly leaning on mantlepiece. It takes a moment for him to catch his breath.* NORMA, *concerned, follows him.*) She locked the window too. I had to climb in through a strange bedroom. There may be a lawsuit.

(*He weakly charges back into the bedroom, followed by*

NORMA, *who grabs his coattails in an effort to stop him. The RAIN outside stops.*)

NORMA. (*Stopping him below bed.*) Don't yell at her. Don't get her more upset.

ROY. (*Turning back to her.*) Don't get her *upset?* I'm hanging seven stories from a gargoyle in a pouring rain and you want me to worry about *her?* . . . You know what she's doing in there? She's playing with her false eyelashes. (*Moves to bathroom door.*) I'm out there fighting for my life with pigeons and she's playing with eyelashes . . . (*Crossing back to* NORMA.) I already made up my mind. The minute I get my hands on her, I'm gonna kill her. (*Moves back to door.*) Once I show them the wedding bills, no jury on earth would convict me . . . And if by some miracle she survives, let there be no talk of weddings . . . She can go into a convent. (*Slowly moving back to* NORMA *below bed.*) Let her become a librarian with thick glasses and a pencil in her hair, I'm not paying for any more cancelled weddings . . . (*Working himself up into a frenzy, he rushes to the table by the armchair and grabs up some newspapers.*) Now get her out of there or I start to burn these newspapers and smoke her out.

(NORMA *stops him, soothes him, and manages to get him calmed down. She gently seats him on the foot of the bed.*)

NORMA. (*Really frightened.*) I'll get her out! I'll get her out! (*She crosses to door and knocks.*) Mimsey! Mimsey, please! (*She knocks harder and harder.*) Mimsey, you want to destroy a family? You want a scandal? You want a story in the Daily News? . . . Is that what you want? Is it? . . . Open this door! *Open it!* (*She bangs very hard, then stops and turns to* ROY.) Promise you won't get hysterical.

ROY. What did you do? (*Turns wearily to her.*)

NORMA. I broke my diamond ring.

Roy. (*Letting the papers fall from his hand.*) Your good diamond ring?

Norma. How many do I have?

Roy. (*Yells through door.*) Hey, you with the false eyelashes! (*Getting up and moving to door.*) . . . You want to see a broken diamond ring? You want to see eighteen hundred dollars worth of crushed baguets? . . . (*He grabs* Norma's *hand and holds it to keyhole.*) Here! Here! *This* is a wor^thless family heirloom— (*Kicks door.*) and *this* is a diamond bathroom door! (*Controlling himself. To* Norma.) Do you know what I'm going to do now? Do you have any idea? (Norma *puts her hand to her mouth, afraid to hear.* Roy *moves away from door to far side of bed.*) I'm going to wash my hands of the entire Eisler-Hubley wedding. You can take all the Eislers and all ^the hors d'oeuvres and go to Central Park and have an eight thousand dollar picnic . . . (*Stops and turns back to* Norma.) I'm going down to the Oak Room with my broken arm, with my drenched rented ripped suit—and I'm gonna get blind! . . . I don't mean drunk, I mean totally blind . . . (*Erupting with great vehemence.*) because I don't want to see you or your crazy daughter again, if I live to be a thousand.

(*He turns and rushes from bedroom, through the living room to the front door. As he tries to open it,* Norma *catches up to him, grabs his tail coat and pulls him back into the room.*)

Norma. That's right. Run out on me. Run out on your daugh^ter. Run out on everybody just when they need you.

Roy. You don't need me. You need a rhinoceros wi^th a blow torch—because no one else can get into that bathroom.

Norma. (*With rising emotion.*) I'll tell you who can get into that bathroom. Someone with love and understanding. Someone who cares about that poor kid who's going through some terrible decision now and needs help. Help that only *you* can give her and that *I* can give her. *That's* who can get into that bathroom now.

(Roy *looks at her solemnly. Then he crosses past her, hesitates and looks back at her, and then goes into the bedroom and to the bathroom door.* Norma *follows him back in. He turns and looks at* Norma *again. Then he knocks gently on the door and speaks softly and with some tenderness.*)

Roy. Mimsey! . . . This is Daddy . . . Is something wrong, dear? . . . (*He looks back at* Norma, *who nods encouragement, happy about his new turn in character. Then he turns back to door.*) I want to help you, darling. Mother and I both do. But how can we help you if you won't talk to us? Mimsey, can you hear me? (*There is no answer. He looks back at* Norma.)

Norma. (*At far side of bed.*) Maybe she's too choked up to talk..

Roy. (*Through door.*) Mimsey, if you can hear me, knock twice for yes, once for no. (*There are two KNOCKS on the door. They look at each other encouragingly.*) Good. Good . . . Now, Mimsey, we want to ask you a very, very important question. Do you want to marry Borden or don't you?

(*They wait anxiously for the answer. We hear one KNOCK, a pause, then another KNOCK.*)

Norma. (*Happily.*) She said yes.

Roy. (*Despondently.*) She said no. (*Moves away from door to foot of bed.*)

Norma. It was two knocks. Two knocks is yes. She wants to marry him.

Roy. It wasn't a double knock yes. It was two single "no" knocks. She doesn't want to marry him.

Norma. Don't tell me she doesn't want to marry him. I heard her distinctly knock "yes." She went— (*Knocks twice on foot of bed.*) "Yes, I want to marry him."

Roy. It wasn't— (*Knocks twice on foot of bed.*) It was— (*Knocks once on foot of bed.*) and then another— (*Knocks once more on foot of bed.*) That's "no," twice, she's not marrying him. (*Sinks down on side of bed.*)

Norma. (*Crossing to door.*) Ask her again. (*Into door.*) Mimsey, what did you say? Yes or no? (*They listen. We hear two distinct loud KNOCKS. Norma turns to Roy.*) All right? There it is in plain English . . . You never *could* talk to your own daughter. (*Moves away from door.*)

Roy. (*Getting up wearily and moving to door.*) Mimsey this is not a good way to have a conversation. You're gonna hurt your knuckles . . . Won't you come out and talk to us? . . . Mimsey?

Norma. (*Leads Roy gently to foot of bed.*) Don't you understand, it's probably something she can't discuss with her father. There are times a daughter wants to be alone with her mother. (*Sits Roy down on foot of bed, and crosses back to door.*) Mimsey, do you want me to come in there and talk to you, just the two of us, sweetheart? Tell me, darling, is that what you want? (*There is no reply. A strip of TOILET PAPER appears from under the bathroom door. Roy notices it, pushes Norma aside, bends down, picks it up and reads it:*) What? What does it say? (*Roy solemnly hands it to her. Norma reads it aloud:*) "I would rather talk to Daddy." (*Norma is crushed.*)

(*He looks at her sympathetically. We hear the bathroom DOOR unlock. Roy doesn't quite know what to say to Norma. He gives her a quick hug.*)

Roy. I—I'll try not to be too long.

(*He opens the door and goes in, closing it behind him, quietly. Norma, still with the strip of paper in her hand, walks slowly and sadly to the foot of the bed and sits. She looks glumly down at the paper.*)

Norma. (*Aloud.*) "I would rather talk to Daddy" . . .

Did she have to write it on this kind of paper? (*She wads up paper.*) Well—maybe I didn't do my best . . . I thought we had such a good relationship . . . Friends. Everyone thought we were friends, not mother and daughter . . . I tried to do everything right . . . I tried to teach her that there could be more than just love between a mother and daughter . . . There can be trust and respect and friendship and understanding . . . (*Getting angry, she turns and yells towards the closed door.*) Just because *I* don't speak to my mother doesn't mean *we* can't be different! (*She wipes eyes with the paper.*)

(*The bathroom door opens. A solemn* ROY *steps out, and the door closes and locks behind him. He deliberately buttons his coat and crosses to the bedroom phone, wordlessly.* NORMA *has not taken her eyes off him. The pause seems interminable.*)

ROY. (*Into phone.*) The Green Room, please . . . Mr. Borden Eisler. Thank you. (*He waits.*)

NORMA. (*Getting up from the bed.*) I'm gonna have to guess, is that it? . . . It's so bad you can't even tell me . . . Words can't form in your mouth, it's so horrible, right? . . . Come on, I'm a strong person, Roy. Tell me quickly, I'll get over it . . .

ROY. (*Into phone.*) Borden? Mr. Hubley . . . Can you come up to 719? . . . Yes, now . . . (*He hangs up and gestures for* NORMA *to follow him. He crosses into living room and down to the ottoman, where he sits.* NORMA *follows and stands waiting behind him. Finally:*) She wanted to talk to me because she couldn't bear to say it to both of us at the same time . . . The reason she's locked herself in the bathroom . . . is she's afraid.

NORMA. Afraid? What is she afraid of? That Borden doesn't love her?

ROY. Not that Borden doesn't love her.

NORMA. That she doesn't love Borden?

ROY. Not that she doesn't love Borden.

NORMA. Then what is she afraid of?

ROY. . . . She's afraid of what they're going to become.

NORMA. I don't understand.

ROY. Think about it.

NORMA. (*Crossing above sofa.*) What's there to think about? What are they going to become? They love each other, they'll get married, they'll have children, they'll grow older, they'll become like us— (*Comes the dawn. Stops by the side of the sofa and turns back to* ROY.) I never thought about that.

ROY. Makes you stop and think, doesn't it?

NORMA. I don't think we're so bad, do you? . . . All right, so we yell and scream a little. So we fight and curse and aggravate each other. So you blame me for being a lousy mother and I accuse you of being a rotten husband. It doesn't mean we're not happy . . . does it? . . . (*Her voice rising.*) Well? . . . Does it? . . .

ROY. (*Looks at her.*) She wants something better. (*The DOORBELL rings. He crosses to open the door.* NORMA *follows.*) Hello, Borden.

BORDEN. (*Stepping into room.*) Hi.

NORMA. Hello, darling.

ROY. (*Gravely.*) Borden, you're an intelligent young man, I'm not going to beat around the bush. We have a serious problem on our hands.

BORDEN. How so?

ROY. Mimsey—is worried. Worried about your future together. About the whole institution of marriage. We've tried to allay her fears, but obviously we haven't been a very good example. It seems you're the only one who can communicate with her. She's locked herself in the bathroom and is not coming out . . . It's up to you now.

(*Without a word,* BORDEN *crosses below the sofa and up to the bedroom, through the bedroom below the bed and right up to the bathroom door. He knocks.*)

BORDEN. Mimsey? . . . This is Borden . . . Cool it!

(*Then he turns and crosses back to the living room. Crossing above the sofa, he passes the* HUBLEYS *and without looking at them, says:*) See you downstairs! (*He exits without showing any more emotion.*)

(*The* HUBLEYS *stare after him as he closes the door. But then the bathroom door opens and* NORMA *and* ROY *slowly turn to it as* MIMSEY, *a beautiful bride, in a formal wedding gown, with veil, comes out.*)

MIMSEY. I'm ready now!

(NORMA *turns and moves into the bedroom towards her.* ROY *follows slowly, shaking his head in amazement.*)

ROY. *Now* you're ready? *Now* you come out?
NORMA. (*Admiring* MIMSEY.) Roy, please—
ROY. (*Getting angry, leans in to her over the bed.*) I break every bone in my body and you come out for "Cool it"?
NORMA. (*Pushing* MIMSEY *towards* ROY.) You're beautiful, darling. Walk with your father, I want to look at both of you.
ROY. (*Fuming. As she takes his arm, to* NORMA.) That's how he communicates? That's the brilliant understanding between two people? "Cool it?"
NORMA. (*Gathering up* MIMSEY'S *train as they move towards the living room.*) Roy, don't start in.
ROY. What kind of a person is that to let your daughter marry?

(*They stop above sofa.* MIMSEY *takes bridal bouquet from table behind sofa, while* NORMA *puts on her wrap and takes her gloves from the back of the sofa.*)

NORMA. Roy, don't aggravate me. I'm warning you, don't spoil this day for me.
ROY. Kids today don't care. Not like they did in my day.

NORMA. Walk. Will you walk? In five minutes he'll marry one of the flower girls. Will you walk?

(MIMSEY *takes* ROY *by the arm and they move to the door, as* NORMA *follows*.)

ROY. (*Turning back to* NORMA.) Crazy. I must be out of my mind, a boy like that. (*Opens door.*) She was better off in the bathroom. You hear me? Better off in the bathroom . . .

(*They are out the door.*)

CURTAIN

PROPERTY PLOT

ACT ONE

ON STAGE:

LIVING ROOM:

Mantel
  On:
    Clock, c.
    2 vases, R. and L.
Fireplace
  In:
    2 brass andirons
    Logs
Front door closed—2 signs on inside knob
Living room draperies open
Living room curtains closed
All window shades one-third down
Desk in bay window
  On:
    Lamp, U. R.
    Ashtray, D. R.
    Stack of envelopes, D. R.
    2 standing cards, U. R. and U. L.
    4 postcards, C.
    2 long service cards, L.
Desk chair, under desk
Waste basket (urn), R. of desk
Mirror, over chest of drawers
Chest of drawers, R. of U. C. window
  On:
    Telephone, R.
    Lamp, R.
    Promenade magazine, C.
    Stack of stationery, L.
      Under—Paper airplane, one-half complete
U. C. window, open 16″
Carpet piece, under U. C. window
U. C. chair, armless
Poof, D. C.
Small carpet, under coffee table
Coffee table, D. S. of sofa

On:
    Ashtray, c.
    Matches, c.
    Long service card, R.
Sofa
  On:
    Pillow, R.
Arm chair, D. R.
Table, U. S. of sofa
  On:
    Crystal vase, empty, R.
    Silver tray, L.
      On—2 crystal decanters
c. door, closed

BEDROOM :

  Bedroom draperies, open
  Bedroom curtains, closed
  Bedroom window shades one-third down
  Waste basket, R. of vanity table
  Vanity table
    On:
      Lamp, R.
      Long service card, R.
      Mirror, c.
      Ashtray, L.
      Matches, L.
      Standing card, L.
    In:
      Standby hair brush, top L. drawer
  Vanity chair, under vanity table
  Chest of drawers, D. S. of c. door
  Luggage rack, D. S. of chest
  Arm chair, U. S. position, D. S. of luggage rack
  Small table, U. S. of arm chair
    On:
      Ashtray
      Matches
      Opaline box, lower shelf
  Right night table

On:
    Lamp
    Telephone
    Note pad
In:
    Gideon Bible, top drawer
Bed
  On:
    Bedspread
    Bolster
    2 pillows
Left night table
  On:
    Lamp
    Ashtray
    Matches
    Valet card

CLOSET:

4 wooden hangers
Door closed

BATHROOM:

Wash basin
  On:
    Glass, three-quarters full water
U. S. towel rack
  On:
    White bath towel
D. S. towel rack
  On:
    2 hand towels
    1 wash cloth
Wastebasket, D. S. of wash basin
Door closed

PROP TABLE—RIGHT:

Overnight bag—BELLBOY
Room key—BELLBOY

Striped box—KAREN
  In:
    Black negligee
    White tissue paper
Dozen white roses, wrapped in green tissue—KAREN
Makeup case—KAREN
  In:
    Hairbrush, top
    Assorted bottles, tubes, jars
Black attaché case—SAM
  In:
    3 blue contracts, bottom
    2 military hair brushes
    Eye drops
    Electric razor
    Bottle of pills
    Black toilet kit, open
      In—Bottle of Jade East
Paper case—JEAN
  In:
    3 blue contracts
    Pantel pen
Newspaper—JEAN
Rolling table—WAITER
  On:
    White table cloth
    1 knife, 2 forks, 3 spoons
    2 white napkins
    Silver tray
      On—White paper doily, hors d'oeuvres and anchovy
            patties
    Silver coffee pot with coffee
    2 coffee cups and saucers
    Silver creamer
    Silver sugar bowl with sugar packets
    Plate with lettuce and sliced tomatoes
    Plate
      On—Saucer with half grapefruit in bowl
    Silver covered platter with sliced roast beef
    Salt shaker
    Pepper shaker

Check (bill)
Pantel pen
2 glasses of water with ice cubes
Silver tray—WAITER
   On:
      Silver champagne bucket
        In—Bottle champagne wrapped in white napkin
      2 champagne glasses

PERSONAL PROPS:

Black purse—KAREN
   In—2 $1.00 bills, lipstick
Wrist watch—SAM
Wrist watch—JEAN
Pillbox with saccharine tablets—JEAN
Glasses—JEAN

END OF ACT ONE

STRIKE:
Rolling table
Tray with champagne and glasses
Vase of flowers from desk
Stationery from chest
Promenade from chest to coffee table
Paper airplane from floor
Room key from chest
Karen's purse from sofa table
Coffee cup from coffee table
Makeup case from vanity table
Hair brush from vanity table
Hair piece from vanity table
Negligee from top drawer, bedroom chest
Striped box from bedroom wastebasket
Tissue paper from bedroom wastebasket
Lipstick from small bedroom table
Glass from right night table
Overnight bag from luggage rack
Karen's mink coat from closet
Notepad from right night table
Bobby pins from right night table drawer

Recharge razor

ACT TWO

ON STAGE:

LIVING ROOM:

Front door closed—2 signs on inside knob
Desk, in bay window
   On:
     Magnum of champagne, L.
     Gold box of candy, R.
     Long white flower box, D. S.
     2 fruit baskets, U. S.
Desk chair
   On:
     White tennis sweater
     Tennis racquet, leaning on floor, in cover
Chest of drawers, R. of U. C. window
   On:
     Check (bill), D. R.
     Pantel pen, D. R.
     3 Old Fashioned glasses, L.
     3 tall glasses, R.
     Telephone, U. R.
     Lamp, U. R.
     Ice bucket, D. R.
       In—Ice cubes
     Vodka bottle with liquid, top off, R.
     Creme de menthe bottle with liquid, top off, L.
     Scotch bottle with liquid, U. L.
     Gin bottle with liquid
     Bourbon bottle with liquid
     Glass mixing pitcher, D. L.
       In—Glass stirring rod
Table, U. S. of sofa
   On:
     3 scripts, blue script on top, open, R.
     Silver tray, L.
       On—2 crystal decanters
Coffee table, D. S. of sofa
   On:
     Promenade magazine, L.
     Ashtray, C.

Matches, c.
Long service card, r.
Center door, open

BEDROOM :

Vanity chair
  On:
    2 neckties
    Blue sweater, JESSE
Chest of drawers, d. s. of c. door
  On:
    1 script, u. s.
    3 books, stacked
    1 blue shirt, folded, d. s.
      On—2 neckties
    Portable tape recorder, d. s.
Golf club, on floor d. s. of chest
Luggage rack
  On:
    2 clothes boxes, top one open
      In—Yellow shirt, in top box
Arm chair, u. s. position
  On:
    Funny papers, u. s. arm
    Blue jacket, d. s. arm
Right night table
  On:
    Lamp
    Telephone
    Brown leather appointment book
Newspapers, on floor, d. s. of r. night table
Bed
  On:
    4 scripts
    Stack of galley proofs
    1 copy "Daily Variety"
    1 copy "Hollywood Reporter"

BATHROOM :

Door open
Pajama tops on doorknob

Towels readjusted
Bottle of shaving lotion on wash basin

PERSONAL:

Cartier wrist watch—JESSE
Purse—MURIEL
  In:
    Compact
    Kleenex

END OF ACT TWO

STRIKE:
3 glasses from coffee table
2 fruit baskets from desk
Magnum from desk
Flower box from desk
Candy box from desk
Tennis racquet from desk chair
Tennis sweater from desk chair
Vodka bottle from sofa table
Bottles from bar
Ice bucket from bar
Glasses from bar
Mixer and stirring rod from bar
Funnies from vanity table
Script from bedroom chest
3 books from bedroom chest
Shirt and 2 neckties from bedroom chest
Portable recorder from bedroom chest
Appointment book from R. night table
Scripts, galley proofs, 2 trade papers and newspapers from
    under bed
Cologne from R. night table
Golf club from D. S. of bedroom chest
2 boxes with yellow shirt from luggage rack
Blue jacket from bedroom chair
Opaline box, ashtray and matches from bedroom table
2 neckties from vanity chair
Pajama tops from bathroom doorknob
3 scripts from sofa table
Muriel's coat, purse and gloves from D. R. chair

ACT THREE

ON STAGE:

LIVING ROOM:

  2 telegrams, U. S. on mantel
  Front door closed—2 signs on inside knob
  Living room drapes full open
  2 center bay window curtains 6″ open
  All window shades one-quarter down
  Desk, in bay window
    On:
      Lamp, U. R.
      Ashtray, D. R.
      Stack of envelopes, D. R.
      2 standing cards, U. R. and U. L.
      4 postcards, C.
      2 long service cards, L.
      Crystal vase, C.
        In—Flower arrangement
  Basket of mums, on floor L. of desk
  U. C. chair
    On:
      Long box of flowers, open
  Coffee table
    On:
      Long box of flowers, open, L.
      Stack of telegrams, C.
      Ashtray, C.
      Matches, C.
      Long service card, R.
      Silver vase of flowers, R.
  D. R. armchair
    On:
      2 sections of newspapers, bridal section on top
  Sofa
  Norma's mink stole and gloves, L.
    On:
      Pillow, R.
  Table, U. S. of sofa
    On:
      Bridal bouquet on white tissue, stems R.
      Silver tray
        On—2 crystal decanters
  Center door open

BEDROOM:

Chest of drawers, D. S. of C. door
  On:
    Man's hat box, U. S.
    Roy's gray gloves, U. S.
    Silver tray, D. S.
      On—Coffee pot, sugar bowl, creamer, coffee cup and
        saucer, spoon, napkin
    Norma's purse, D. S.
      In—Tissues
Luggage rack
  On:
    Large white dress box, open
      In—Gold skirt, over D. S. edge
Brown suitcase, on floor D. S. of rack
  On:
    Brown sweater
Bedroom chair, turned to D. S. position
Small table, turned to D. S. position
  On:
    2 sections of newspaper
Right night table
  On:
    Lamp
    Telephone
    Coffee cup and saucer
Bed
  On:
    Newspapers, bridal sections, U. R.
    Roy's blue suit, U. L.

BATHROOM:

Lock door with bar
Wash basin
  On:
    Note on 4-square length of double-ply toilet tissue
      On—"I would rather talk to Daddy" in light lipstick
OFF LEFT:
Bucket of warm water

PERSONAL:

Diamond ring—NORMA

COSTUME PLOT

ACT ONE

BELLBOY:
Plaza Hotel Bellboy Jacket, Navy
Plaza Hotel Bellboy Trousers, Navy
White shirt
Black bow tie
Black shoes
Black socks
Gold vest

KAREN:
Dark red 2 piece suit, rhinestone pin on jacket
Pink blouse
Body padding
Touque tights
Black pumps
Black alligator purse
Black kid gloves
Plastic galoshes
Mink hat
Mink coat
Wedding band
Hair piece

SAM:
3 piece brown glen plaid suit
Light blue shirt
Paisley necktie
Brown suspenders
Brown shoes
Brown socks
Black overcoat

WAITER:
Navy trousers
White waiter jacket with red epaulets
White shirt
Black bow tie
Black shoes
Black socks

JEAN:
Brown skirt
Orchid blouse
Bone shoes
Natural tights
Pink suede coat
Brown velvet beret with wooden pin on
Brown purse
Brown gloves
Brown fall

ACT TWO

WAITER:
Same as Act One

JESSE:
Aqua suede trousers
Beige turtle neck sweater
Blue coat sweater
Brown socks
Brown buckle shoes
Blond wig

MURIEL:
Gray wool dress
Black patent leather shoes
Black beaded purse
White gloves
Yellow coat
Tan tights
Red fall
Wedding band

ACT THREE

NORMA:
Green lace dress
Green net hat
White mink stole
White kid gloves
White sequin evening bag
Pearl necklace
Diamond ring
Charcoal stockings
Streaked hair piece

ROY:

Morning trousers
Black tails
White wing collar shirt with cufflinks
Gray ascot
Gray half vest
Carnation in lapel
Black socks
Black shoes
Gray wig

BORDEN:

Morning trousers
Black tails
White wing collar shirt with cufflinks
Gray ascot
Gray half vest
Carnation in lapel
Black socks
Black shoes

MIMSEY:

White wedding dress with train
White tulle headpiece
White pumps
White kid gloves
Flesh tights

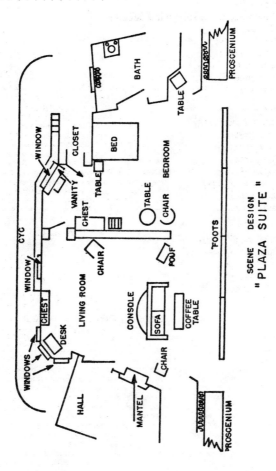

SCENE DESIGN
"PLAZA SUITE"

Other Publications for Your Interest

GROWN UPS
(LITTLE THEATRE—COMEDY)
By JULES FEIFFER

2 men, 3 women, 1 female child—Interiors

An acerbic comedy by the famed cartoonist and author of *Knock Knock* and *Little Murders*. It's about a middle-aged journalist who has, at last, grown-up—only to find he's trapped in a world of emotional infants. "A laceratingly funny play about the strangest of human syndromes—the love that kills rather than comforts. Feiffer's vision seems merciless, but its mercy is the fierce comic clarity with which he exposes every conceivable permutation of smooth-tongued cruelty . . . Feiffer constructs a fiendishly complex machine of reciprocal irritation in which Jake (the journalist), his parents, his wife and his sister carp, cavil, harass, hector and finally attack one another with relentless trivia that detonate deeply buried resentments like emotional land mines . . . Moving past Broadway one-liners and easy gags, (Feiffer) makes laughter an adventure . . . This farce is Feiffer's exclusive specialty, and it's never been more harrowingly hilarious."—Newsweek. "Savagely funny."—N.Y. Times. "A compelling, devastating evening of theatre . . . the first adult play of the season."—Women's Wear Daily.   (#9125)

LUNCH HOUR
(LITTLE THEATRE—COMEDY)
By JEAN KERR

3 men, 2 women—Interior

Never has Jean Kerr's wit had a keener edge or her comic sense more peaks of merriment than in this clever confection, starring Gilda Radner and Sam Waterston as a pair whose spouses are having an affair, and who have to counter by inventing an affair of their own. He, ironically, is a marriage counsellor, and a bit of a stick. His wife juggles husband, lover and mother and is a real go-getter. In fact, it was she who proposed to him. Of the other couple, the wife is a bit kooky. She can discourse on things tacky while wearing an evening gown with her jogging sneakers on; or, again, be overjoyed at the prospect of a trip to Paris: "And we'll never have to ask for french fried potatoes. They'll just come like that." While her husband, "Well, he's rich for a living." Or as he expresses it: "It's very difficult to do something if you don't need any money." All ends forgivingly for both couples, as the aggrieved wife concedes that they both "need something to regret," and the other husband concedes "I knew when I married that everyone would want to dance with you." "Civilized, charming, stylish . . . Very warm and most amusing . . . delicately interweaves laughter and romance."—N.Y. Times. "An amiable comedy about the eternal quadrangle . . . The author's most entertaining play in years."—N.Y. Daily News. "A beautiful weave of plot, character and laughs . . . It's delicious."—NBC-TV.   (#674)

Other Publications for Your Interest

THE SQUARE ROOT OF LOVE
(ALL GROUPS—FOUR COMEDIES)
By DANIEL MELTZER

1 man, 1 woman—4 Simple interiors

This full-length evening portrays four preludes to love—from youth to old age, from inno-cence to maturity. Best when played by a single actor and actress. **The Square Root of Love.** Two genius-level college students discover that Man (or Woman) does not live by intellectual pursuits alone . . . **A Good Time for a Change.** Our couple are now a suc-cessful executive and her handsome young male secretary. He has decided it's time for a change, and so has she . . . **The Battling Brinkmires.** George and Marsha Brinkmire, a middle-aged couple, have come to Haiti to get a "quickie" divorce. This one has a surprise ending . . . **Waiting For To Go.** We are on a jet waiting to take off for Florida. He's a re-tired plumbing contractor who thinks his life is over—she's a recent widow returning to her home in Hallandale. The play, and the evening, ends with a beginning . . . A success at off-off Broadway's Hunter Playwrights. Requires only minimal settings.   (#21314)

SNOW LEOPARDS
(LITTLE THEATRE—COMIC DRAMA)
By MARTIN JONES

2 women—Exterior

This haunting little gem of a play was a recent crowd-pleaser Off Off Broadway in New York City, produced by the fine StageArts Theatre Co. Set in Lincoln Park Zoo in Chicago in front of the snow leopards' pen, the play tells the story of two sisters from rural West Virginia. When we first meet Sally, she has run away from home to find her big sister Claire June, whose life Up North she has imagined to be filled with all the promise and hopes so lacking Down Home. Turns out, life in the Big City ain't all Sally and C.J. thought it would be: but Sally is going to stay anyway, and try to make her way. "Affecting and carefully crafted . . . a moving piece of work."—New York City Tribune. *Actresses take note*: this play is a treasure trove of scene and monologue material. *Producers take note*: the play may be staged simply and inexpensively.   (#21245)

THIEVES

(LITTLE THEATRE—COMEDY)

By HERB GARDNER

8 men, 3 women—Interior

The hero is Martin Cramer. He lives in an expensive highrise of Manhattan's Upper East Side. He plays Debussy on his balcony at 1 o'clock in the morning. The heroine is Sally Cramer, played with great success in N.Y. by Marlo Thomas. They have been married 12 years. No children, but a load of valuable antiques. They are on point of departure. Their marriage is sliding into the quicksands of early middle-age; two schoolteachers, lost in little New York, surrounded by colorful street people and stereotyped neighbors. She has a darling, old deaf taxidriver for a father, and a young hoodlum as a student (when other pupils bring her an apple, he brings her a stolen t.v.). During the play they both attempt to consummate affairs with other people, but neither succeeds. Eventually they get together after various plot entanglements. " 'Thieves' say more about New York and its people than any play in years. I loved it! "—Leonard Probst, NBC. "Hilarious scenes, marvelous characters and touching moments. One of the better comedies of the season."—WINS Radio.   (#22007)

THE GOODBYE PEOPLE

(LITTLE THEATRE—COMEDY)

By HERB GARDNER

5 men, 1 woman—Exterior

The Goodbye People is a serious comedy about old age and death, but it is also about the woes of youthful misfits and their loves. It is Coney Island in February and Old Max Silverman, recovering from a coronary, is planning to reopen his long-closed beach bar—with the entrapped assistance of his daughter, Nancy, who has changed her name and her nose, deserted her husband and is searching for an identity. Into their dreams and lives wanders Arthur Korman, a youngish, amiable sunrise-watcher who hates his job, but never seems able to make a decision to quit. The three of them together activate their dreams— Arthur quits his job, Nancy decides to divorce her husband and Max will reopen his stand. But in the end, death takes Max, but only after his dream is fulfilled. Milton Berle starred as Max on Broadway. "Milton Berle straight and touching in endearing Herb Gardner Play." —N.Y. Daily News. "His best play."—Jules Feiffer. "Herb Gardner is one of the truly original comic minds in the world. He is also a poet. And *The Goodbye People* is one of the most truly comic stage poems you will ever see."—Paddy Chayevsky.   (#9078)

Other Publications for Your Interest

SOCIAL SECURITY
(LITTLE THEATRE—COMEDY)

By ANDREW BERGMAN

3 men, 3 women—Interior

This is a real, honest-to-goodness hit Broadway comedy, as in the Good Old Days of Broadway. Written by one of Hollywood's top comedy screenwriters ("Blazing Saddles" and "The Inlaws") and directed by the great Mike Nichols, this hilarious comedy starred Marlo Thomas and Ron Silver as a married couple who are art dealers. Their domestic tranquility is shattered upon the arrival of the wife's goody-goody nerd of a sister, her up-tight CPA husband and her Archetypal Jewish Mother. They are there to try to save their college student daughter from the horrors of living only for sex. The comic sparks really begin to fly when the mother hits it off with the elderly minimalist artist who is the art dealers' best client! "Just when you were beginning to think you were never going to laugh again on Broadway, along comes *Social Security* and you realize, with a rising feeling of joy, that it is once more safe to giggle in the streets. Indeed, you can laugh out loud, joyfully, with, as it were, social security, for the play is a hoot, and better yet, a sophisticated, even civilized hoot."—NY Post. (#21255)

ALONE TOGETHER
(LITTLE THEATRE—COMEDY)

By LAWRENCE ROMAN

4 men, 2 women—Interior

Remember those wonderful Broadway comedies of the fifties and sixties, such as *Never Too Late* and *Take Her, She's Mine*? This new comedy by the author of *Under the Yum Yum Tree* is firmly in that tradition. Although not a hit with Broadway's jaded critics, *Alone Together* was a delight with audiences. On Broadway Janis Paige and Kevin McCarthy played a middle aged couple whose children have finally left the nest. They are now alone together—but not for long. All three sons come charging back home after experiencing some Hard Knocks in the Real World—and Mom and Dad have quite a time pushing them out of the house so they can once again be *alone together*. "Mr. Roman is a fast man with a funny line."—Chr. Sci. Mon. "A charmer."—Calgary Sunday Sun. "An amiable comedy . . . the audience roared with recognition, pleasure and amusement."—Gannett Westchester Newsp. "Delightfully wise and witty." Hollywood Reporter. "One of the funniest shows we've seen in ages."—Herald-News. TV. (#238)

Other Publications for Your Interest

ALONE AT THE BEACH
(LITTLE THEATRE—COMEDY)
By RICHARD DRESSER

4 men, 3 women—Combination Interior/Exterior

"So you thought the kind of comedy that sends audiences home happy had disappeared from the American theatre scene? *"Wrong!"* enthused the Louisville Courier-Journal over this literate, witty comedy, which had the audience at Actors Theatre of Louisville's famed Humana Festival whooping with laughter. George, a mild-mannered man in his mid-30's, has inherited a beach house in the Hamptons on Long Island. In order to afford to keep it, he has let out rooms to boarders, Manhattan-ites desparate to get out of the city on weekends. Blindly, and blithely, George has not actually *met* any of these denizens of the yuppie sector of the urban jungle. If everyone were Great Fun and Easy To Get Along With, everyone would have a great time—but the audience, of course, wouldn't. Who wants to watch a bunch of friendly, well-adjusted people have Fun In The Sun? Thankfully, Dresser gives us a motley crew of urban neurotics, male and female, who begin to drive George, and everyone else, crazy the moment they arrive. Somehow, though, everyone survives the experience, egos intact; and, in fact, some of the most unlikely romances develop, before everyone has to face reality: Labor Day and, subsequently, the trek back to New York City for good—until next summer? "Has a unique sparkle." New Albany Tribune. "A winner...a riotously funny sex farce."—Detroit News. "A charming romp that should turn up in regional and community theatres all over the place."—Houston Post. "Has the pacing of a Neil Simon script but with some of the dry, more cerebral wit of Jules Feiffer."—Evansville Courier.

(#3118)

EMILY
(ADVANCED GROUPS—SERIOUS COMEDY)
By STEPHEN METCALFE

8 men, 4 women, to play a variety of roles.
Bare stage, w/drops, wings, projections & wagons; or, may be unit set.

This brilliant, cynical, contemporary new comedy by the author of *Strange Snow, Vikings, Sorrows and Sons* and *The Incredibly Famous Willy Rivers* dares to take what amounts to a politically "incorrect" stance about the successful "New Woman." Emily is a successful New York City stockbroker who mixes it up with the boys and always comes out on top. In fact, she was described by one misguided critic as coming off like a "man in drag"; because, as we all know, women are caring, loving, nurturing creatures—and what a wonderful world it would be if *they* were in positions of political and/or business power, instead of those insensitive jerks, the *men*. Emily is just as cynical and ruthless as any man in her position; until, that is, she meets a caring, sensitive, aspiring actor (in other words, a nice guy with no money) who doesn't fall for her manipulative ruses; but, rather, for the real Emily he sees inside the ruthless yuppie—who may, or may not, exist. "Glorious...a sparkling comedy with bite to it. The title character is a gold mine of a role for an actress."—San Diego Tribune. "A real winner...a bravura balancing act right on the edge of sentimentality, finally and triumphantly crystalline in its emotional honesty...A triumph." —San Diego Union.

(#7076)